Summerlings

ALSO BY LISA HOWORTH

Flying Shoes

Summerlings

Lisa Howorth

DOUBLEDAY
New York

 Published in the United States by Doubleday, a division of Penguin Random House LLC, New York, and distributed in Canada by Random House of Canada, a division of Penguin Random House Canada Limited, Toronto.

www.doubleday.com

Grateful acknowledgment is made to the following for permission to reprint previously published material:

Hal Leonard LLC: Lyric excerpt from "Three Cool Cats," words and music by Jerry Lieber and Mike Stoller, copyright © 1959 by Sony/ATV Music Publishing LLC, copyright renewed. All rights administered by Sony/ATV Music Publishing. International copyright secured. All rights reserved. Lyric excerpt from "The Twelfth of Never," words by Paul Francis Webster and music by Jerry Livingston, copyright © 1956 and renewed by Webster Music Co. and Hallmark Music Company. All rights for Hallmark Music Company controlled and administered by Spirit Two Music, Inc. International copyright secured. All rights reserved. Reprinted by permission of Hal Leonard LLC. New Directions Publishing Corp.: Excerpt from "Canto LXXXI" from *The Pisan Cantos,* copyright © 1948 by Ezra Pound. Reprinted by permission of New Directions Publishing Corp.

A portion of this work first appeared as "Ode to Chesapeake Bay" in the August/September 2017 issue of *Garden & Gun.*

Library of Congress Cataloging-in-Publication Data

Names: Howorth, Lisa, author.
Title: Summerlings : a novel / Lisa Howorth.
Description: New York : Doubleday, 2019.
Identifiers: LCCN 2018053370 (print) | LCCN 2019002780 (ebook) |
ISBN 9780385544658 (ebook) | ISBN 9780385544641 (hardcover)
Subjects: | BISAC: FICTION / Historical. |
FICTION / Literary. | GSAFD: Bildungsromans.
Classification: LCC PS3608.O95729 (ebook) |
LCC PS3608.O95729 S86 2019 (print) | DDC 813/.6—dc23
LC record available at https://lccn.loc.gov/2018053370

Front-of-jacket photographs: boy © The Advertising Archives/Alamy Stock Photo; spider © Domiciano Pablo Romero Franco/Alamy Stock Photo
Jacket design John A. Fontana

MANUFACTURED IN THE UNITED STATES OF AMERICA

1 3 5 7 9 10 8 6 4 2

First Edition

For Washington, my four Washingtonian grandparents,
and all the grandparents who save the day

"Dear, sweet, unforgettable childhood!"

—Anton Chekhov,
"The Bishop"

Summerlings

I

For us boys, the summer of 1959 was as cataclysmic as a meteor. Washington's historic plague, our wild neighborhood party, and my first acquaintance with death—these are the things I remember so vividly from that bright season, along with the accompanying feelings of fear, revelation, and wonder.

I was eight, the time in life when everything is still new, and some things are perceived clearly but others are murky and not understood—that is to say, those things in the realm of adults. What my friends and I knew was a grab bag of information overheard, along with information we made up and told one another and accepted as fact. Not really so different from the grown-up world, I suppose. We existed in a smaller world of our own daunting challenges, peopled with gods and monsters. Sometimes they were the same.

It was a scorchingly hot summer. Maybe the record-high temperatures had something to do with our plague. But Washington summers are always fairly hot; the city is built on a swamp, after all. What were L'Enfant and Banneker thinking? Paris, I suppose. Wide diagonal boulevards, circles, obelisks, bronze and granite heroes—but built on marshy land where cattle once grazed.

The city grew like a swamp, too. Our neighborhood, just over the District line near Chevy Chase Circle on Connecticut Avenue, was lushly green in summer, even deep into August. Connors Lane, originally just a farm road, was jungly and mossy—Virginia creeper and ivy grew on houses, grass grew from cracks in the sidewalk and street. Few people had perfectly tended yards, or exotic nursery specimens from Johnson's Flowers or American Plant Food. What grew was what was used to growing: boxwoods, dogwoods, oaks, holly and yew, maples and mulberries, and, of course, the iconic cherry trees, although they weren't indigenous and had been given to the city of Washington by the Japanese government in 1912. My mother told us that when the Japanese bombed Pearl Harbor, an angry mob set the cherry trees at the Japanese embassy on fire. But cherries thrived all over the city—their delicate pink blossoms so very lovely in spring, giving our stolid, stony city a lighter feel, like a frill of petticoat peeking from under a nun's habit. In our old neighborhood, steps and walks crumbled and mold grew on walls. We didn't worry about things like mold back then; we worried about polio and radioactivity. The big oaks created a dense canopy on our lane—a tunnel where we boys foraged and loitered and ran amok like the little beasts that we were. The light under the canopy gave everything a dark, watery green cast in summer, a green not like any of the greens in my new box of sixty-four Crayolas.

—

Connors Lane had been part of a large farm established in 1848 by two Irish immigrant brothers of that name. The farm had been sold, although a remnant of the family still lived down the lane, toward Western Avenue, where most of the newer houses were. Some of those new houses belonged to second-generation Jewish couples whose parents or grandparents had escaped Europe before the Holocaust. My grandfather said our neighborhood, because it wasn't part of the more "hoity-toity enclave" closer to Connecticut Avenue, was one of the few places in Chevy Chase where Jews were allowed to live, which I didn't understand but was told not to talk about. Our end of the lane, close to Brookville Road, consisted of mostly older houses of assorted vintages. My grandmother called us the "Whitman's Sampler" because our neighbors were all so different, and from "somewhere else." Other countries, but also from other places in the U.S. Not unusual for the Washington area, but, looking back, it was unusual for most of America. We certainly didn't think it was different then; as far as we knew, it was just like everywhere else. Everywhere else must have diplomats, government people, and refugees from one bad thing or another, is what we thought, if we thought about it at all.

In fact, our family were the oddballs—Washington natives, although, of course, originally we were from "somewhere else," too. My grandfather Brickie's grandfather, a Schultze, had come from Germany (Brickie wasn't especially proud of this) and made harnesses for President Taft's horses. Poor horses! Brickie's mother came from Limerick, and my grandmother Dimma's people were from

Philadelphia, going way back. I didn't know as much about my dad's family because he and my mother divorced when I was five or so, and things were not cordial between them. My sister, Liz, and I didn't see our father often: the occasional dinner at O'Donnell's Sea Grill, or the Touchdown Club, and we'd go with him to Rehoboth Beach for a few days every summer. Daddy's family, Mannixes, were Irish, too, and Catholic—"mackerel snappers," as the lapsed-Catholic Brickie said, and I did know that Daddy had worked with his father in real estate, but they'd had a falling-out over some slum properties my father didn't want to deal with. He still hadn't found a job. Brickie said my dad was allergic to work.

We called my grandfather "Brickie," a nickname from his sandlot baseball days on the Ellipse, and because of his bright-red hair. His real name was John, same as mine. He worked down in Foggy Bottom for the United States Information Agency, writing broadcasts for Voice of America. He also helped create the Jazz Ambassadors program, sending famous jazz musicians around the world to make people like America. My grandmother Dimma's name was a child's corruption of "Dear Ma," what *her* grandmother had been called. Dimma did lady things: played bridge, shopped for beautiful clothes, did a little charity work, and enjoyed the crossword puzzle in the morning *Washington Post* with her Chesterfields and Cutty Sark. She was still pretty, her hair a subtle gold, and she wore stylish cat-eye glasses to match. Brickie and Dimma came to live with us when my parents separated.

Our house was fairly modest, a three-story brick colonial

array of mostly international families. The De Haans lived next door in a big new house shoehorned onto a lot too close to ours, according to my grandparents. The De Haans were Dutch and had two boys, Kees and Piet. I didn't play with them much because they didn't go to Rosemary School with me but to Beauvoir—a school where Europeans sent their children who were in danger of becoming too American. Kees and Piet dressed nicely and were opposed to getting dirty, which didn't sit too well with me and my two best friends, Max and Ivan. Max had heard his dad say that General de Haan had been a Nazi sympathizer during World War II. I couldn't understand why, if he was the enemy, he hadn't been hanged or shot by a firing squad and was living freely in America, but apparently it was the fault of "lily-livered, bleeding-heart eggheads" like Adlai Stevenson, according to the father of the Shreve boys down the street. The General was tall, with an imposing gut, and dressed impeccably in wool vests and velvety moleskin pants, even in summer. Like Kees and Piet, he slicked back his hair, which in his case only accentuated his baldness. I never saw him smile. They'd built a small, ridiculously blue swimming pool—very unusual for Chevy Chase back then—and it was *wunderbar,* but Max was never invited to swim because he was Jewish, and then we were *all* banished for something atrocious we'd done to Kees and Piet to get back at them for excluding Max. We deeply regretted what we did, or so I said in an apology note Dimma had made me hand-deliver, but mainly our regret had to do with not being allowed in their pool. My grandmother occasionally had tea with

Madame de Haan, who had crammed their house with lovely old European antiques "No doubt *acquired* from their Jewish neighbors," Brickie said. But Dimma enjoyed their Old World culture and felt sorry for Madame. "She must be twenty years younger than he is," she told my grandfather. "He doesn't even let her drive."

"Of course he doesn't," Brickie said. "Because she would drive the hell *away*. Just like, I might add, those one hundred thousand Dutch Jews who would've liked to."

The Friedmanns, Max's family, on the other side of the De Haans, didn't want Max playing with Piet and Kees, even though the Dutch boys were polite and much better behaved than Max and Ivan and I were. The Friedmanns had escaped Austria before the war, after the Anschluss. They lived in a brownish, decrepit farmhouse that was cool and dim inside and smelled like pineapple. I thought this was because Mrs. Friedmann baked a lot, maybe with special Jewish ingredients, but Dimma said that the aroma was due to "lax housekeeping." I'd pointed out that at least it didn't reek of Clorox and ammonia, like our house after our maid, Estelle, cleaned. Things were just old and worn out. The Friedmanns were kind of poor by our neighborhood's standards because they'd had to leave everything behind when they fled Austria. The nicest things in the house were the handsome bookshelves Mr. Friedmann had built to hold their many books, some of which were in Hebrew. Mr. Friedmann had been an electrical engineer in Austria, but now tuned pianos and fixed clocks and radios and tended a huge vegetable garden in their backyard. Mrs. Friedmann wore peasant skirts and kept her salt-and-pepper hair in a long braid down her back. She went to a lot of meetings at their synagogue, Adas Israel in Cleveland Park, and read newspapers in other languages, like Esperanto. Brickie called them "beatniks, but without the jazz and poetry." But he occasionally helped Mr. Friedmann with his garden, and loaned him records. In return we got delicious tomatoes, and sometimes his prized watermatoes; a successful experiment in crossing cherry tomatoes with watermelons. Their tabby cat was named Wiesie, for Simon Wiesenthal, because, as Max said, "She stalks and executes mice like Wiesenthal with the Nazis." Since Max was going on ten, a year older than Ivan and I, he liked to be the authority on things, and his much older sister was a rich repository of teenage wisdom. Max informed us about things like how babies were made, and born, which was so disturbing it couldn't possibly be true. He also knew what queers did—*mate with guys*—doubly unimaginable.

In the house beyond the Friedmanns lived an ancient spinster, Miss Prudence Braddock, neighborhood doyenne by virtue of being one of the original inhabitants on Connors Lane before the farm had been divided up and sold off. We never saw her and we were told to leave her alone and stay out of her yard—she didn't like children, possibly because our baseballs often threatened her spectacular lavender azaleas, which were as ancient as she was and as big as rooms. She owned a magnificent dollhouse full of tiny, precious furnishings she'd collected over her long lifetime. Dimma and my mother had been invited to see it, but not Liz, still deemed a kid, nor our Brazilian friend, Beatriz—Miss Braddock didn't like foreigners, either. Beatriz didn't really care, but my sister was sorely disappointed and she vowed to break into Miss Braddock's to get a look. "She's mean, and she's going to die any minute, anyway," Liz said. And eventually die she did, and the dollhouse went to the Smithsonian, without any of us children ever getting a look.

The Andersens lived on the other side of us. Mr. Andersen was an artist; I don't know why they lived in Washington, or where they'd come from. They were very "modern," Dimma said, not admiringly; their immaculate Craftsman home featured a carefully tended yard, new Danish furniture, and a ferocious charcoal-colored Giant Schnauzer named Foggy, who we believed was mainly there to keep us off their property. Even though he was behind a fence, we were terrified of him—he hated all living things but especially us, possibly because we often threw magnolia-pod hand grenades at him. Once we'd seen him eat a box turtle whole, like it was a chocolate-chip cookie, and a regrettable thing had happened not too long before involving the Shreves' cat and Estelle, our maid. Dimma believed the Andersens looked down on us as *déclassé,* and she declared that they "put on airs," and were "dour," which I took to mean boring, but they had spectacular arguments that were anything but. There was an angry daughter a little younger than Liz—Maari—who was even scarier than my sister. Max and Ivan and I had once seen Maari break a baseball bat when she was emphasizing where she thought home plate should be, and this was so impressive we steered clear of her. And there was a three-year-old we called Punchy Jane because she held her hands in fists and worked her elbows fiercely when she walked.

Next to the Andersens were the Wormy Chappaquas, so-called because they'd given me worms, or at least Dimma decided they had, possibly because their skin was a dark gray. They were new to Connors Lane from a place called Chappaqua, which we decided must be an Indian reservation, maybe explaining their skin color. We didn't play with the three girls because they were girls, and too young, but we were intrigued with what they referred to as the Mess: a tiny car with all kinds of strange gadgets. It had only three wheels and opened from the front. My grandfather said it was made from the nose gear of a German Messerschmitt warplane, and, "Who in hell would want to drive around in a piece of crap like that? How many people were *killed* by that thing?" We would have loved to drive it around, and I guess I got the worms from them the one time we went over there and tried to bully the girls into letting us play Sputnik in it. Brickie said we'd be traitors if we played in it, and Mr. Friedmann told Max he agreed. It's possible they were kidding, but we took it to heart.

At the corner of Connors and Brookville was the Pond Lady, whose yard, tangled with vines, featured a brown pond that obsessed us, although, like Miss Braddock's yard, the pond was off-limits to us. Of course, this hadn't stopped us from twice sneaking in to meddle with the pond creatures, most notably an albino frog we named Peachy because of his pale, rosy body, which we could see through. His insides looked like M&M's. We'd gotten caught last time by Josephine, the Pond Lady's helper, who yelled at us but never told on us, maybe because she and Estelle were friends. The Pond Lady lived in an iron lung that we were keen to get a gander at—I'd described it to Max and Ivan as similar to a personal-size submarine or a coffin, based on a terrifying movie my dad took me to see—*The Monolith Monsters*—in which a lady was in an iron lung because of some radioactive meteorites. Brickie said the Pond Lady wrote spy books that were "grossly inaccurate," but because she was British, Dimma approved of her—the piece in the Whitman's Sampler filled with Nut Honey Caramel, as opposed to the weirder Liquid Pineapples.

Beatriz's family, the Montebiancos, lived on the corner opposite the Pond Lady. Senhor Montebianco was some kind of cultural attaché at the Brazilian embassy and worked with museums and galleries around Washington. He was extremely handsome, and I got the same wiggly feeling seeing him as I did watching Clipper on *Sky King,* or Mary Martin *and* Cyril Ritchard in *Peter Pan*—I loved their tights. Senhor Montebianco wore slim, beautiful suits, and smiled warmly with big white teeth like piano keys. Sometimes he smelled faintly of something like my grandmother's Shalimar, but how could that be? We played with Beatriz, "an unbridled tomboy," according to Dimma, who liked her in spite of this because she had nice manners that might rub off on me. She was Max's age, and smart, funny, and tough. Beatriz didn't go to school with us, but to Visitation, a Catholic girls' school down in Georgetown. She had to wear a navy-blue uniform and her shiny black hair in long pigtails, so Max sometimes called her "Little White Dove," from "Running Bear," a popular song we boys liked. The Montebiancos were very religious. Brickie didn't seem suspicious of them, although I'd heard him say to Dimma, "At least they're not more goddamn Reds," to which Dimma had replied, "That's enough, John. *Little pitchers.*" Every morning, when we began our trek to Rosemary School, a good mile away, the Senhor, Beatriz, and her older brother went off in their Mercury Montclair, the Senhor and Beatriz waving enthusiastically and calling, "*Oi! Tchau!* See you later!"

The Shreves lived in a small, newish house next to the Montebiancos and across the lane from the Chappaquas. They were from Louisiana—*Shreveport,* they liked to point out—and they might as well have been from another country, too. We had more trouble understanding Mrs. Shreve than we did our foreign neighbors. We didn't have a lot in common with the Shreve boys, Beau and Davis Lee, called D.L., and, although we sometimes played together, we were intimidated by them. They went to Bullis Prep and were mainly interested in baseball—playing it, as well as following the Senators and the team from where their dad had gone to college, a place the boys referred to as "Ella Shoe." The Shreve boys believed that the Montebiancos had probably

Goncharoffs seemed fairly well-off, and Elena often took Max, Ivan, Beatriz, and me to movies at the Hiser, to get ice cream at Gifford's, or on outings to Glen Echo amusement park, where she would ride on the hair-raising white roller coaster with us, not the pink one that chickens like Ivan and I preferred. Of course we loved her! Josef—Ivan called his father by his first name, and we were allowed to, too—had been ambassador to Mexico but was now "between assignments," according to Ivan, who thought it was because his father had a heart condition. Brickie put it another way: He'd been "recalled" by President Eisenhower for "some *unpleasantness.*" Josef and Elena, brother and sister, had come to America from the Ukraine when they were young, to get away from Stalin, but even so, the Soviet connection didn't endear Josef to my grandparents. Or at least that's what I thought, although their misgivings might have been about Elena, about whom I'd overheard Brickie say, "consorts with unsavory refugees." Because of all that, Brickie and Dimma didn't like us hanging around the Goncharoffs', but they liked us hanging around *our* house even less. They approved of Ivan, though, because he was sweet, quiet, and studious—and I think they may have felt sorry for him. Josef and Elena didn't get along at all; they had loud, disturbing arguments. Ivan didn't get along with his father, either—he never wanted me and Max to come over if Josef was home. Luckily, he was not around much and was often away for a week or two. Ivan's mother had taught Spanish at B-CC, the local high school, but she'd died after having Ivan's younger brother and sister, twins, and that was when Josef had

Allgood's brother had died at Utah Beach. Brickie had been in the army, too, though not in combat—he had specialized in linguistics and spent time in England and Latin America. There must have been a point in the early fifties, around the time we boys were born, when everyone was relieved that the war was over and optimistic about peace. But things had ratcheted up again with the Soviet Union humiliating us in the space race, having spy rings that cracked the Manhattan Project, and now they had the Bomb. Khrushchev had already vowed, *"We will bury you!"* and, earlier that summer, visiting Moscow, Nixon had angrily poked him in the chest. In retaliation, Khrushchev had said he was going to do everything he could to help defeat Nixon in the 1960 election, which infuriated Brickie: "The very goddamn idea of those bastards interfering in our elections!" And, of course, right after Christmas, there'd been the Cuban revolution, Castro bringing Communism within ninety miles of the U.S. There was a lot of fear in America. Everyone believed that there was a very good chance that the world would soon blow up. At school we practiced three scary civil-defense drills for different attack scenarios, but even we boys knew that Washington would be the first place annihilated, and nobody would survive. So the Cold War caused our neighbors to be nervous and suspicious of one another. Who you were, where you had been, and what you had done during World War II set boundaries, and for Ivan and Max and me, this meant things often got in the way of our having fun. On those broiling August days when we could hear Kees and Piet splashing and yelling happily in their pool, we wanted badly to be invited to swim again and for Max to be included. We wanted to get in the Wormy Chappaquas' Messerschmitt without feeling like traitors. We wanted to be able to hang around with Elena as much as she'd let us, even if she did consort with unsavory refugees. And, though it had nothing to do with the war, we wanted to get a look at the Pond Lady's iron lung. We wanted what *we* wanted first, but we also simply wanted everybody to get along. Why couldn't our neighborhood be more like Beaver Cleaver's, where people were nice to each other?

We hoped to fix things. Taking our cue from the Marshall Plan, which we vaguely knew from our *Weekly Reader*s was a plan to help reunite Europe, we came up with our Beaver Plan. Of course, we had no idea of how we'd accomplish neighborhood reunification, but if we could enlist the help of our goddess, we knew we'd find a way. And it was a good excuse to spend more time with her.

2

Ivan and I started our summer mornings as if we had a job we had to do, and we would report to Max's front porch and wait quietly for Max to get up. This particular morning, we'd intended to discuss the Beaver Plan, but Ivan and I had woken to find all the yards up and down the lane festooned with clouds of spiderwebs. Hedges were frosted with them, and in the trees overhanging the lane, the webs looked like strings of crystal beads lit with dewdrops that sparkled spectacularly in the early sun, connecting all the yards, as if the neighborhood were one big carnival. Ivan and I were beside ourselves, hollering like maniacs under Max's window until he busted out of his house in nothing but his underpants.

"Can you believe this?" I shouted at him.

"Man, oh man!" he yelled. "How did this happen?"

Some webs stretched horizontally between trees that were a good thirty feet apart, and some soared way above our heads, like the gossamer riggings of a ghost ship.

"How do they *do* that?" Ivan said.

I was clutching the front of my shorts, an unfortunate

habit when I was extremely excited. Ivan was spinning around, taking it all in. "There are *thousands* of them! Maybe *millions*!"

"Do you see any actual spiders?" Max called. "Let's catch them!" He raced over to the privet hedges in front of the porch. "Here's one! A *big* one with yellow stripes! His web has a sort of zipper thing right down the middle! Here's another one!"

Mrs. Friedmann stepped out from behind the screen door in her robe. "Vaht's all the commotion?" she demanded. "It's only seven o'clock!"

"Mutter, spiders are everywhere!" Max shouted. "Look down the street!"

"Oy gevalt!" she exclaimed, shaking her head with a hand to her mouth. "Your fahzer is not going to like zis. Max, come inside and put some clothes on!"

"Rats!" He ran back inside.

Ivan and I continued around the yard, examining the wild profusion of spiders easily within our grasp. Like tiny nets of diamonds, the webs even covered the scrubby lawn.

"Here's one with a huge butt!"

"There's a big moth stuck in this web and he's wrapped like a mummy! He's still moving!"

Max emerged with shorts on, carrying some jars. "C'mon! We can have an instant collection before anybody else!"

"Boys! Zhey might be poison! Do not bring zhem into zhe house!" Mrs. Friedmann shuddered and went back inside.

"Look at this one, you guys!" Max cried. "He looks just like a tiny crab!" He fiddled with a jar, trapping it.

Just then, Beatriz came squealing up the lane, waving her arms. "Boys, boys! What *is* this? Look what happened to me!" She was alarmed but laughing, her head and shoulders veiled with webs.

But just as we all began twirling into the nearest webs, laughing and winding ourselves like spools of thread in the gluey, silken lines, Beatriz screamed, "Help! A spider went down my blouse!" She danced around frantically until something big and black fell out of her shirt, and the spider ran to a hole in the ground and disappeared. "Ick! The webs are fun, but I don't want any spiders on my personal body."

Max, still twirling, guffawed and said, "I guess that spider was a sex maniac and wanted to see your bosoms!" He was always saying stuff like that to Beatriz, to either get her attention or annoy her, I wasn't sure.

Beatriz said back, "I don't have any bosoms, Max, so shut up and stop talking about bosoms all the time." Max just laughed.

Ivan had fallen to his knees to examine the hole. "Wow—do some spiders live in the ground?"

Mr. Friedmann shouted from inside the house, "Don't go near zhe garden today, kids. I'm going to put poison on zhe wegetables to kill zhe spiders."

"Not even a spider would want to eat his flabby eggplants," Max said. Mr. Friedmann had so many eggplants in his garden that the family ate them every night, to Max's disgust. "Yech. They taste like fried flip-flops."

Ivan, abandoning the spider hole and wiping his hands on his shorts, said, "These webs are too itchy. Let's wash off in the hose." Ivan was often itchy. Max pulled a hose around from the side of the house, squirted himself, and Ivan and I stripped off our sticky, sweaty T-shirts and he hosed off the two of us.

Beatriz, still on the sidewalk, watched. "What about you, Beatriz?" Max said, grinning; his little wet nipples pinched up from the cold water.

She said, "*As if!* See you guys later." She flounced off home. If one can flounce in polka-dot short-shorts.

We were in hog heaven. We liked spiders but didn't know a lot about them, though, of course, we'd all read *Charlotte's Web* and loved it. But Max and Ivan and I were rabid collectors, and this spider plague opened up new collecting opportunities. Past summers it had been rocks, fossils, and shark teeth from the Chesapeake Bay, and then snakes, although we gave that up because snakes presented too many problems: Ivan the Tenderhearted cried about the little pink-and-white mice we had to feed them, so he started to liberate his mice in the house, which hadn't gone over well with Maria, and one of my garter snakes had gotten out and just about given Estelle a heart attack—the only time she'd ever threatened to quit. And there was an unsettling event at the Friedmanns' involving Max's sister and his queen snake.

Most recently we'd gotten into butterflies. Max and I had our favorites—buckeyes, red admirals, various swallowtails, and question marks—along with some obligatory blues, painted ladies, and sulphurs pinned to boards in our rooms, and a few colorful, spiky caterpillars. Ivan didn't have many because they were so beautiful he couldn't bear to kill them, and he was more interested in studying their behavior anyway.

He was an excellent observer, and, following his lead, we made it our business to find out everything there was to know about whatever we collected—or at least everything there was to be found in our little pocket *Golden Guides,* or, the ultimate authority, Brickie's *Encyclopaedia Britannica.* We also ransacked the rickety green bookmobile that parked every Thursday in front of Doc's pharmacy on Brookville Road, but they didn't have much. Sometimes we nagged Elena until she took us to the National Museum, its monumental presence on the Mall a holy shrine to us boys, stuffed with sacred relics in the form of dinosaurs, gems, fossils, insects, and butterflies that we could worship, and covet, up close. So we already knew some things about insects, making the shift from butterflies to spiders a natural progression.

"Spiders aren't *insects,* you know," Ivan pointed out, always the smartest of us. "I think they're arthropods, like crabs and lobsters. And I *think* scorpions, too, maybe?"

"Then can people eat *all* arthropods?" I asked. "We could make a spider stew and get Beau and D.L. to eat some. Or Slutcheon!" Slutcheon was an older kid we hated and feared. He lived on Quincy, one of those "hoity-toity" streets several blocks away. Slutcheon was so bad he made the Shreve boys look angelic in comparison.

Max said, "Yeah! Slutcheon! Maybe we could make him sick. Or *die.*"

"Yeah, the Shreves eat those crappy *crawdads* all the time," I said, faking a gag. To us, crawdads were crayfish, small, pale creatures we found in the sandy bottom of Rock Creek, a Potomac tributary that wound its way through the wooded parts of Northwest Washington, a few blocks from us. Estelle had said that crawdads were eaten only by "crazy white folks." She was not a big fan of the Shreve boys and didn't like them coming around our house.

"It would be funny to see Beau and D.L. eat spiders, but not as much fun as killing Slutcheon," Max said.

Ivan was ruminating on this. "If we killed anybody we'd have to go to reform school." He was always so practical. "But if we just make somebody sick, we might get away with it. Let's just catch every kind of cool spider we can."

"We can take them to school and everybody will be jealous of us," I said.

"Yeah, and we can scare girls with them," Max added, inspired as always by visions of mayhem. Girls weren't afraid of butterflies, but they would be of spiders. I was thinking of how horrified my sister, Liz, would be to find one in her pillowcase. I'd have to make this happen before she went off to boarding school.

"And if we mess Slutcheon up, maybe he'll leave us alone," Max added darkly.

"Or maybe he'll want revenge and kill us," I said.

Max looked at me contemptuously. "Don't be such a chicken! Gah!"

"Takes one to know one," I said, unfazed. Max wasn't

really mean. He and I both were regularly beaten down by our older sisters, so I understood his need to assert his seniority over me and Ivan.

Ivan, ignoring the bickering, said, "We have to figure out how to catch the poisonous ones. Our butterfly nets won't work with them because we can't touch those." We'd figure something out—we always did, the way we figured out how to kill the gnats that drove us nuts every day by taking my grandfather's giant world atlas, holding it open in a gnat cloud, and slamming it shut on them. Of course, Brickie yelled at me when he went to use the atlas and its pages were stuck together with gnat bodies. Then we resorted to making a flamethrower with Dimma's Aqua Net hairspray and Max's matches, which annihilated whole swarms of gnats in seconds.

Ivan said, "Let's do some research!" We liked to do research. It's what Brickie spent a lot of time doing. It felt important and scientific. We spread our books out in my living room. Normally, we would have done this on the Goncharoffs' wide front porch, in hopes of Elena coming out and joining in, but Ivan said doubtfully, "Josef's home today. He'll just bother us." And if Josef was home, chances were that Elena wouldn't be.

Dimma came through the living room, still in her robe. "These spiders are simply horrid," she said. "I've never seen anything like it in all my life." She looked down to see what we were reading. "Good Lord! Don't even think about it!"

"We're not, Dimma," I said. "We're just doing research

about them, so we can find out how to get rid of them for you."

"If I find you bringing any spiders into this house, I'll be doing research on how to get rid of *you*. That snake was bad enough."

We giggled but made no reply. She said, "You heard me!" and went off in a Chesterfield cloud. Estelle came through in her crisp white uniform, dragging the Hoover. We greeted her, always polite to keep in her good graces, but I protested, "Estelle, we're doing something important here."

"Important—hmpf!" she huffed. "It cain't be as 'portant as me gettin' my work done. How I'm gone vacuum in here with y'all all sprawled out?"

"Can you do it later? *Please?*" I beseeched her. "We're trying to figure out how to get rid of the spiders."

"You're not foolin' nobody!" She began lugging the Hoover away. Then she turned to us and said, in a sonorous voice: *"Y'all act with hostility against me and unwillin' to obey me, I'm gone increase the plague on you seven times 'cordin' to your sins."* She moved off, laughing and muttering to herself about snakes, bugs, and boys.

"Did you hear that! *Seven times* as many spiders!" Ivan said.

"That's just some Bible stuff," Max said. "The Bible always talks about plagues." We went back to our work, happily discussing spider facts until Estelle returned and evicted us. But we'd found what we needed; we had our list of the poisonous spiders we intended to trap: black widows, brown recluses, and tarantulas.

Over the next few days Estelle's prophecy came true. *The Washington Post* and *The Evening Star* reported on what was apparently a citywide spider infestation. Not content with festooning the streets, spiders were now *inside* people's houses, offices, and cars, making all the grown-ups crazy. The papers said that experts weren't certain why it was happening. There was speculation that it was the unusually hot weather, or less rain, or more smog, or, because some of the spiders being found weren't native to the Washington area, that immigrants and refugees were bringing them in. (Max had been right: Scorpions were being found, and we added them to our list.) Brickie had his own theory—*insect warfare.* He might have been kidding; sometimes it was hard to tell. But however they got to Washington, spiders *were* everywhere: in shops, restaurants, trains, and planes. It was all people talked about. They were in corners, dressers, mailboxes, pots and pans, pianos, bookshelves, lampshades, and shower stalls. Everyone walked around thrashing and sputtering through the webs, which hung invisibly in doorways and stairwells and clung to faces, arms, and knees. Estelle reported it was the same down in Southeast DC, where she lived, and that the bus she rode to work was full of spiders and webs, "An' people lookin' like lunatics tryin' to keep 'em off!" When Estelle arrived at our house those mornings, Dimma helped her check her clothing for spiders, and plucked webs off Estelle's sleekly curled hair. Then when Dimma came back from an outing, Estelle did the same for her. They both were terrified of spiders.

Brickie and I were having breakfast when he told me he'd found a brown recluse in a file drawer in his office. He was not happy about it, to put it mildly. He had his face in the *Post,* drinking his morning coffee. I was trying to eat the scrambled egg he made me every day. "Eating a good breakfast is like lighting a fire: It will keep you going for the rest of the day" was Brickie's credo. One of many. But I'd already eaten two bowls of Frosted Flakes before he was even up.

"Did you see the little violin on his back?" I asked, slamming down my juice glass in excitement.

Not looking up, he said, "No, because I immediately smashed the hell out of it."

"Gah, Brickie! You could have caught him for me! We *need* a brown recluse!"

Brickie lowered his paper and peered at me thoughtfully over his reading glasses. "Sometimes I wonder about you, son." He went back to the paper.

"Why do you think it's happening, Brickie?" I ate some scrambled egg—now cold—and spit it back on my plate. "And if you didn't see his violin, it might not have been a brown recluse."

"We don't know what's going on. *Yet.* I have a theory, though, and if I find one more damn spider in my office we're going to see World War Three. It *was* a brown recluse because the lab said it was."

"Why do you have a *lab* at your office?" I couldn't imagine why there would be a lab at the USIA office. "You think some Russian spies are doing it?"

"The lab is not in *my* office, it's . . . just close by," he said. "Russians have a long tradition of poisoning their enemies. In fact, they have a place called Laboratory 12 where that's all they do—figure out how to poison people." He looked at me again. "Don't leave the table until you finish your breakfast—every bite."

"There's a common house spider up in that corner, over your head," I said. "At least I *think* that's all it is."

While Brickie craned his head to look, I took the opportunity to scrape my cold egg onto the floor. "Jesus Christ. Estelle! Can you come in here, please?" he called.

Estelle appeared with a broom and dustpan and quickly knocked the web down, stepped on the spider, and swept it up. "Thank you," Brickie said. She spotted the egg on the floor and swept that up, too, giving me a look. "Uhm, uhm, uhm," she said, and bustled off.

"Why doesn't anybody just *ask* the Russians if they're doing it? Don't they always love to brag about stuff?"

Brickie snorted. "John, the Soviet idea of truth is very different from ours. They call their newspaper *Pravda,* which is Russian for 'truth,' and it's nothing but propaganda. They lie to their own people, which is something we'd never do in America. Russians are the greatest storytellers on earth. They can't help but lie."

I squirmed in my chair, desperate to get away and report Brickie's news to the boys, so I stuffed the last corner of toast into my mouth and washed it down with the last of my orange juice. "Well, if the Russians were trying to get you they would put more than one brown recluse in your office because just one bite probably wouldn't kill you unless your 'health is already comprofied,'" I said, trying to quote from the *Britannica.*

Brickie sighed. "That word is *compromised.* And my office has been thoroughly sprayed now."

He made a dismissive sound. "This conversation is over. You're excused."

I hopped up and tried to run off but was intercepted in the hall by Dimma, who said, "John, don't put your feet in your shoes without checking! Don't put an arm through a sleeve or your leg through your pants without shaking them thoroughly! Look between the cushions before you sit on the sofa! Check the drawers! Check your toys! And *don't* collect any of them!"

"We decided to be exterminators, Dimma. We're going to hunt them and kill them. You should be glad." A lie, of course. I went on, "Also, spiders are actually good because they eat roaches and mosquitoes and moths."

Recognizing a lost cause, Dimma said, "Is that right, Otto the Orkin Man? Just as long as you kill them and keep them out of the house. *Please* be extremely careful, and wear gloves. Your mother won't appreciate it if you die of a spider bite."

Calling on our research, I said smartly, "Since 1950, only fourteen-point-one percent of bites from vemonous insects were lethal. Most bites won't kill anybody. They might make you sick, or your arm might rot off, but that's all."

"Oh, I see. I guess your mother would be okay with that,"

she said sarcastically. "It's pronounced *ve-no-mous.*" Then, always her last words, "And *you heard me*!"

Ivan and Max were on the Friedmanns' bottom step, waiting on me, for a change. Ivan was idly turning over rocks. A daddy longlegs and a few roly-polies were under a concrete chunk and Max picked them up, wrapped them in a piece of Popsicle trash, and stashed it in his pocket to feed Tallulah Flathead, the yellow queen snake whose head had been stepped on and mangled a little bit by his sister. For some reason Tallulah refused to die but loved to eat.

I blurted out what Brickie had said, or what I'd decided he'd said: "Brickie thinks the Russians planted all the spiders to poison everybody in Washington!"

"Really?" Max exclaimed. Then he asked skeptically, "How does he know that?"

"Um, I'm not sure. I guess he knows people who know." I looked apologetically at Ivan. "And he said Russians are the biggest liars on earth."

"We're not Russian. We're Ukrainian," Ivan corrected. "And not all Russians lie—I think just the government."

Max said, "Well, Russian *and* Ukrainian people hate Jews, and tell lies about them all the time."

I was getting confused about all of this—Soviets, Russians, Ukrainians, and why did everybody hate Jews?—and I said, "Let's not talk about that stuff."

"Yeah," said Ivan. "Let's just collect spiders."

After gathering some peanut butter and mayonnaise jars from Max's kitchen, we went over to the old stable behind my house, which seemed like the perfect place for spiders to hide, particularly up in the hayloft, with its crumbling rafters. After a couple hours of scrounging, we hadn't caught much. One or two good specimens—a leopard-legged silver argiope in a zigzag web, and a wolf spider under some bricks—but mostly it was the same boring spiders we didn't care about. We hadn't even glimpsed anything dangerous. It was dawning on us that spider-collecting was tougher than we'd expected—hot, sticky, and frustrating, with mosquitoes, flies, and gnats feasting on us.

"It must be nine thousand degrees up here!" Max complained. "I quit!" He began descending the ladder.

"Yeah, me, too," Ivan said, clambering behind him. "Too bad we're not collecting horseflies."

"I know," I said, sighing. "The spiders in here sure aren't doing much to kill all these stupid mosquitoes, either."

"These butterfly jars are too big to carry around," Max said. "And how are we going to keep the grown-ups from seeing the spiders, since we're keeping them alive?"

We thought. Then Ivan said, "I know! Prescription bottles! We catch them in those, because nobody will notice them in our pockets. And we transfer them to jars to keep." This seemed like a good idea to me and Max, although we said the grown-ups would kill us if they found them. It was decided that Ivan would keep them, because no one was paying much attention at his house.

There were plenty of pill bottles around all our houses; mostly for Miltown, the most popular of the new "Mother's Little Helper" drugs, which I'd seen advertised for the "tense and nervous patient." My mother had certainly been tense and nervous, and she'd had the pills for as long as I could remember, but it surprised me that Dimma, Mrs. Friedmann, and Elena took Miltown, too. But I'd also seen the drug recommended for a disease called *menopause,* so I thought that maybe Dimma and Mrs. Friedmann had that. Elena had even more Miltowns than my mother. She said they helped with her asthma, but she still suffered from attacks, and always carried her inhaler with the pills.

Feeling better about things, we gathered up all the Miltown bottles we could find, putting nail holes in the tops. Max and I had orangey pill bottles and Ivan had Elena's green ones, from Mexico. We were set, but we knew that the spiders would die soon, and, unlike Charlotte, they wouldn't be leaving babies behind because of all the DDT the newspapers said was being marshaled against them. We'd have to find our prize spiders fast. School would start in a couple weeks.

3

A few days later, we were in my kitchen slapping together some potato-chip sandwiches: take two pieces of Wonder Bread, slather them with Miracle Whip, place a fistful of Wise potato chips on one slice, put the other on top, and mash down firmly. Estelle frowned upon this, so we sneaked them up to my room. After dispatching the sandwiches, we were lying on my twin bed in front of the fan, depressed because we still hadn't found a poisonous spider. We had a crablike spiny orb weaver, and Max had *thought* he'd seen a scorpion, but it had skittered away under his porch. We knew Wiesie was too smart to mess with it.

"And we haven't done anything about the Beaver Plan yet," Ivan said.

"You mean the plan to get invited to the De Haans' swimming pool," Max said sarcastically. My bedroom window was open, and we were tortured by the sounds of the Dutch boys enjoying a refreshing swim.

"Anybody got an idea?" Ivan said.

"Nope," Max said. "The only idea in *my* head is to pee in that pool if I ever get in."

"What about presents for everybody to make them like us?" I asked. "Like maybe mounted butterflies?" I'd mounted a handsome zebra swallowtail and sent it to my mother. "We're through with them, right?"

"No! I don't want to give any of mine away!" Max complained.

"Plants?" I said. "We can pick Brickie's peace roses and put them in Dixie cups? *Peace,* get it?"

Ivan said to Max, "Or maybe your dad will give us some of his watermatoes to give out?"

"He's not going to do that," Max said. "Plus, there wouldn't be enough to go around."

"What if we did drawings for everybody?" Ivan offered. "Like maybe"—he paused—"what if we drew maps of our street? With everybody's houses looking nice?" This excited him—he was good at drawing.

"Nah," said Max. "John and I are bad drawers and nobody will want ours."

I said, "Is Elena home yet, Ivan?" She'd been visiting "friends" in Miami for one of her projects; I wondered if they were unsavory refugees.

"She just got home this morning, but she might be asleep. She was tired."

We spilled out of my house, but not before stealing some Twinkies from the kitchen, which we stopped to eat, hiding in the porte cochere behind Dimma's Cadillac. Crossing the street, we were delighted to see that Elena had taken up her usual spot on the long swing on Ivan's front porch.

Elena spied us and lifted a long arm to wave. "Come see

me!" she called. We ran up the lichen-covered concrete steps to where Elena reclined on her side, so exotically regal—an earthy Madame Récamier. Her shiny hair was tied back with a blue scarf, a long cascade falling down the back of the silky flowered kimono she wore all day because she didn't have to go anywhere. "My job is going to parties!" she'd say—and that's what she did many nights. Her brilliant red toes and fingernails—Sports Car, she said the color was called—always gave me a thrill, a new color every few days. I felt a kind of wiggliness about Elena, too, and was confused about it.

Ivan leaned over, kissed his aunt, and asked, "Is he back yet?"

"His flight doesn't get in until tonight," she said. She was somehow able to hold her usual rum and Coke, a cigarette, and *Carteles,* an arty magazine, in one hand and rub Ivan's back with the other.

"Cuba libre, darlings? It's sooo hot today!" She offered her glass. We always took a swig to refresh ourselves. She handed over her cigarette, a glamorous Vogue, rose with a gilt filter, and we each had a puff. We were, of course, sworn to secrecy. We kept Elena's secrets and she kept ours.

We collapsed worshipfully on the floor in front of her swing. "Elena, we hunted spiders all morning, and we got eaten alive by bugs, and it's about a million degrees!" I whined, thinking about kissing those feet.

"Can we go to the Hiser for a movie?" Max asked. "We're about to have heatstroke!"

Movie theaters were some of the only air-conditioned

places in town then, and luckily for us, Elena was crazy about movies. We had seen *Rodan* and *Go, Johnny, Go!,* but Max complained about some of her choices, like *Auntie Mame,* which she, Ivan, and I had loved. My grandmother also complained about *Mame* because it was "too sophisticated" for us, and was full of "sexual innuendo," but all that went right by me. All I knew was that this handsome orphan, Patrick, lived with his gorgeous, party-girl aunt, who spoiled the hell out of him. Since my own parents were gone, I liked to imagine myself as Patrick and Elena as Mame, living the charmed life in a swanky New York apartment. I suppose both Ivan and I thought of her as a surrogate mother, only more fabulous than any mother we knew of.

"No, Max!" corrected Ivan. "Elena, we need you to help us with our Beaver Plan to make the neighbors nicer!"

She laughed. "Beaver Plan? How'd you come up with *that*?"

"You know, a friendly neighborhood like in *Leave It to Beaver.* Like the Marshall Plan helps countries in Europe be nice to each other," I explained.

"Hmm . . . I see. But you know that some people think that the Marshall Plan is actually more about the United States getting what it wants," Elena said. "Could your Beaver Plan really be about wanting to get in the De Haans' swimming pool again?"

"No, we didn't think about that," I said innocently.

Elena hid the slightest smirk behind her drink, sipping it. "Well, do you have any ideas?"

Max said, "We thought of some dumb stuff, like giving people flowers or drawings, but nothing good."

"What about baking some cookies?"

Ivan said sadly, "We don't know how to cook."

Elena thought for a second, and then said, "How about throwing a neighborhood party? A potluck party, so everybody brings something?"

We looked at one another in amazement. "Yeah! A party!" I shouted. It immediately came to me that maybe my mother, even my dad, might come.

"That's a great idea!" Ivan said. "Like with music and dancing?"

"Sure," said Elena. "Why not? Everybody likes parties, right?"

Max turned serious for a second. "And with good snacks? Like, no vegetables? And *we* don't have to dance, do we?"

"Well, you have to dance with *me,*" Elena said, red lips spreading with her easy laugh.

"Okay!" I loved the dreamy prospect of dancing with her. "Let's do it!"

Ivan asked, "What should we do? Make invitations? I wish Beatriz was here." Beatriz was very creative.

"Well, you have to let everybody know about it. Maybe it would be easier if you just made a few posters and put them up around the neighborhood? But first you have to decide what day and time the party will be, and where. And you might have a name for the party."

I said, "But like what?"

"What about 'Great Big Cool Party'?" Max suggested.

Ivan said, "I think we should have 'Festival' or 'Fiesta' in the name because that sounds more fancy and, umm . . . international."

"What about 'Big Fun Fiesta'?" I said.

"It needs more . . . *oomph,*" Elena said. "And maybe something about families, so people won't think it's just for kids." She pulled out a green pill bottle and her smokes from her kimono sleeve, where she carried important things, popped a Miltown, and lit another Vogue, a lovely turquoise.

"How about 'Fabulous Family Fiesta'?" Ivan looked up hopefully at Elena, who said, "Mmmh!" and enthusiastically blew a plume of smoke into Ivan's upturned face. "That's perfect! I'm sorry, darling—I didn't mean to blow on you." She fanned the smoke away with her hand. Ivan beamed.

I was ready to make the posters right then, but Elena said she had too much to do, and she'd be out the rest of the afternoon and into the evening.

"Rats," said Max. "You go out too much."

"Who are you going out with *this* time?" Ivan asked, not bothering to hide his disappointment.

We knew it could be any number of men. Cars pulled up to the Goncharoffs' at all hours and whisked Elena away to parties at the Fairfax hotel or the Rive Gauche, ritzy spots in town, or a palatial town house in Kalorama or an embassy on Mass. Ave. She often told us about them later—the food, the dancing, the political celebrities, the money they raised for Latin American or European refugees. My grandfather said, "There's nothing more boring than Washington parties," but

I don't think he went to the parties Elena went to. When we slept over at each other's houses and sneaked out to ride bikes in the middle of the night, we'd sometimes see Elena return with a gentleman friend. They'd stagger up to the porch and smoke. Sometimes she didn't come home until daylight, riding in a Diamond Cab, and then there would be a loud argument in Russian with Josef. Air-conditioning and privacy were luxuries few people had in those days, so windows and doors were open, and conversations, especially those that involved shouting, flew around the neighborhood like flies. Unlike flies, you couldn't swat secrets—they buzzed around forever on Connors Lane. From the Andersens we'd heard, "Oh, why don't you go back to Provincetown with your precious little *boyfriend,*" and, "You are the most *vile* harridan I've ever known!" Which sent me straight to my grandmother's crossword puzzle dictionary. Or it might be the Shreves, laying into Beau and D.L. on a regular basis, and Dawn Allgood was known for screaming at her boyfriend. And, of course, before their divorce, there had been my parents.

"It's not really a date," Elena said. "It's more of a meeting." She stubbed out her Vogue in the heavy brass ashtray by her swing, looking with distaste at all of Josef's smelly cigar butts. Josef supposedly had his bad heart and Elena had her asthma, but they both smoked incessantly. "I'm talking to some important people about some Hungarian families who are having trouble staying in the country," she continued. "Your schoolmate Gellert's family is one. So please be glad I'm doing something useful."

We weren't. We liked Gellert okay, a strange kid who was a head taller than Max but was in the same grade at Rosemary as Ivan and I were. He'd come to Washington recently and couldn't speak English and did odd things, like sniff our heads to show appreciation. But he was a lot of fun on the playground at recess, and we always wanted him on our kickball team—he was fast and clobbered the ball, although occasionally he would neglect to round all the bases and would just run way off into the outfield, chasing the ball and laughing. Which didn't matter because he always kicked homers. Even so, I wasn't pleased that he was garnering more of Elena's attention than we were.

"They won't send him back," I said. "This is America."

Elena smiled sadly and said, "Things are not always what they seem, even in America. And sometimes life is terribly unfair."

Just then Linda and Rudo, the Goncharoffs' big poodles, and the naked twins, Katya and Alexander, tumbled out the door. All four of them were covered in spiderwebs and happy about it. Clumsy Rudo, looking like a brown bear, jumped up on the big chair we called The Throne, and Elena scolded him, "Rudo! Get off that chair! You know better!" Apricot-colored Linda, who did know better, flopped on the floor with the twins, looking alarmed. The Throne was Josef's special seat—a handsome rattan thing with huge, poofy cushions covered in a verdant tropical print. Josef had decreed that nobody but he himself was allowed to sit on it. He wanted no dog hair, Popsicle drippings, cigarette holes, and certainly spiderwebs on his cushions when he came out in his robe to smoke his nightly cigar. But I'd seen Elena occasionally sitting on The Throne when a gentleman friend was sprawled on her swing. I wondered if this was ever the cause of their arguments. I wondered, too, if Elena did it just to spite him.

Elena ejected Rudo from The Throne and onto Linda and the twins. She fanned the overheated pile of curly fur and cherubic flesh with her magazine. "Why are you two not taking your nap?" she said to the toddlers, poking them with the Sports Car toes, and the swing swung, making me long to sit close to her. Calling out musically to Maria, "Ma-dee-a!" Elena gave each child a swig of her Cuba libre. Maria appeared and dragged the twins off into the house.

"Can we have another sip?" I asked as Elena rattled her glass.

"No, it's just ice and slobber now." She spilled the ice on the floor for the dogs, who scrambled to lick it up, crunching the melting cubes.

Elena said she had to go upstairs soon to get ready for her appointment. To appease us, she reached into her special sleeve and handed each of us a piece of Bazooka chewing gum, and we shoved the powdery squares into our mouths, chewing out the sugar as fast as we could to then see who could blow the biggest bubbles. Elena flipped through her magazine, then raised her head, listening. "Boys, don't I hear Tim coming?"

Bells jingled far away. Tim was our Good Humor man. His square white truck appeared every summer afternoon but Sunday to deliver succor in the form of Creamsicles, Fudgsicles, Drumsticks, and Popsicles. Elena pulled a dollar bill from the silky sleeve. "My treat!"

Max took the folded bill from her hand and the three of us jumped off the porch and piled into the huge mildewed hammock close to the street to wait.

It had become really, really hot. Our striped T-shirts were soaked, and we took them off. Being crammed into the rough hammock against each other activated our various itchy spots. I had a patch of ringworm healing on my scalp from my rabbit, Zorro, who my grandmother had *supposedly* taken to live with "rabbit friends" at the National Zoo; Max had some scabby impetigo on his knee; and Ivan had poison ivy—he had peed in the weeds at Rock Creek and the end of his penis had swelled up like a doughnut. We always had something scrofulous going on. Ivan had his hand in his pocket so no one could see his furious wiener-scratching. In anticipation of ice cream, he and I spat our Bazooka out, but Max swallowed his. We'd all been told never to do that because gum was indigestible and became a big tumor in your gut. Max considered every piece he swallowed an act of defiance and bravery.

Finally, the Good Humor truck, with its sacred cargo, rounded the corner. The three of us and the dogs ran to the street, busting through new webs that had appeared on the iron front gate during the night, and clustered around Tim, who was swatting gnats. "*I* have the money, and I got here first, punks," said Max, as he and Linda and Rudo pushed in front of me and Ivan.

"We know you are but what are we," Ivan and I said in unison. We loved our snappy comebacks.

"Hey, guys, take it easy!" Tim took off his cap and wiped his sweaty face on his sleeve. He was cute in a clean-cut, military way with his Butch-waxed blond crewcut and white uniform. "What does everybody want?" He glanced up at the Goncharoffs' porch, grinning and waving when he saw Elena. She rose imperially from her swing and was gliding down the walk like she was on wheels.

As Tim gave us our usual Creamsicles and Rainbow Push-Ups, Elena declared that she wanted to try a new feature displayed in a colorful photo on the side of the truck—the Toasted Almond Bar.

"Yours is on me, beautiful," Tim said, handing it to her. Like the rest of us, Tim was chronically infatuated with Elena, and I'd never seen him let her pay for her ice cream.

"Hey, why aren't ours ever on you, too?" Max said, handing over Elena's dollar.

"Because you guys are far from beautiful." He gave Elena a hopeful look. "It's thrilling your mouth, right?"

Elena smiled around a bite of the Toasted Almond Bar. "It *is* delicious!" she purred.

Tim grinned proudly. "I'm glad you like it." Linda and Rudo danced around expectantly. Tim threw them a damaged lime Popsicle and they devoured it, sticks, wrapper, and all.

Max said coyly, watching Tim, "Elena has a date."

Tim smiled. "Damn right she does! I wish she'd give me a try. Can't you put in a good word for me, Ivan?"

"No," Ivan said flatly. "She mostly likes guys from other countries."

"And rich guys," Max added.

"*I'm* rich!" Tim jangled the silver money-changer on his belt. "*And* I always have *good humor.*"

He and Elena chuckled, but Max said, a little sourly, "So funny I forgot to laugh. Maybe you should invent a Cuba libre Popsicle if you want her to love you."

"Maybe I will!" He tipped his cap to her.

"We're going to have a neighborhood party," Ivan announced. "A Fabulous Family Fiesta! Elena's going to help us plan it!"

"Maybe you can come and bring a bunch of Popsicles?" I said. "It's for a good cause . . . It's for . . . uh . . . neighborhood unity!"

"Sure," he said. "I'm always happy to help a pretty lady, even if she hangs around with shrimpy hoods." He and Elena smiled at each other. Elena delicately licked the ice cream off her lips.

Refreshed, we threw our sticks in the road rubble next to the Goncharoffs' rusty front gate.

Elena thanked Tim and said, "We'll let you know more about the party." Looking sternly at us, she added, "And you boys have a lot to figure out—whose parents will host the Fiesta, who'll bring what refreshments, decorations—all that. The party won't just happen on its own. Ivan's right—you need Beatriz helping you." She blew Tim a kiss as she drifted back to the house. Elena didn't exactly sashay; she *je ne sais quoi*–ed in a certain way that later in life I'd try to approximate.

Tim watched her go and sighed. "I'll see you squirts tomorrow. I gotta finish my route and mow some lawns." Tim had several jobs, trying to save money for a car and junior college. His family lived in the apartments down Bradley Boulevard in Bethesda. "You guys don't know how lucky you are." He cruised off down the street, bells ringing in what I thought was a more melancholy way.

"His bells sound sad now," I said.

"His *balls* are sad, too, I bet," crowed Max. Ivan and I laughed, but I knew he and I didn't really get it, so I quit laughing and said, "Why?"

"Aww, forget it, you dumbheads. Don't you guys get *anything*?" Max said.

Often we'd wait for a mob of ants to carry a whole Popsicle stick away while we sang "Song of the Volga Boatmen," but the dogs had ruined that. Then Max said, "Hey, that reminds me! Look what I got!" Out of Max's pocket came a Pep Boys matchbook. "Ivan, gimme your knife." Ivan always carried his little pocketknife. Max quickly poked holes in the matchbook cover and pushed some matches through, making it look like the three Pep Boys had giant dicks sticking out of their pants.

"Oh, *man*!" I said. We cackled like idiots.

"I learned it from this cool guy Frank at Hebrew school," Max said proudly. Then he pulled out another matchbook—he always had matches—and lit the dicks on fire. "This part I figured out myself!" We loved anything involving fire, and there was nothing funnier than jokes involving private parts or bodily functions. Max threw the matchbook on the street, and we were happily watching it burn, when a kid on a shiny new bike turned in to the lane, coming our way.

"Oh, crap!" Max moaned. *"Slutcheon!"*

"Oh, no," I said. "He better not stop."

Slutcheon had a real name, but we called him Slutcheon because he had loose, rubbery lips, drooled a little when he spoke, and had curly hair like Sal Mineo, but not cute—more like a mug shot I'd seen of Lucky Luciano in one of Brickie's books. He was ugly in every sense of the word, and "Slutcheon" just seemed to fit him. It was rumored that Slutcheon had been caught stealing a jar of Peter Pan peanut butter from the DGS, taking it home, pooping in it, and replacing it on the store's shelves. He was rich. We hated him.

"Let's get outta here!" Ivan turned to scramble back to his house, but it was too late, and Slutcheon was upon us, yelling, "Hey, dimwits! How's life on the other side of the tracks?" He zoomed as close as he could, his bike wheels scattering gravel on us. Luckily he kept going, and after he was out of earshot, Max shouted, "Go to hell, you big jerk!"

I said, "Are we on the other side of the tracks? What tracks?"

Ivan said, "He means we're on the poor side of town." I thought "poor" referred to colored people downtown, and Chevy Chase seemed the opposite of that.

"Will he come to the Fiesta?" Ivan asked fearfully.

"Hell, no!" Max barked. Then he spat, adding ominously, "A spider is in that guy's future. If we can just find a good one."

The next afternoon, to our disappointment, Elena was still not around to help us with the Fabulous Family Fiesta posters, and we couldn't find Beatriz. In Max's Big Chief tablet, we had made a perfunctory list of things we needed to be doing—1. CHAIRS 2. TABLES 3. DECORASHONS 4. PUNCH—but had not actually done anything else beyond asking for permission to throw the party in someone's backyard. Mrs. Friedmann declined, citing the likelihood of her husband's garden being trampled, and Ivan didn't want to do it at his house—and we knew Josef wasn't likely to agree anyway. That left Brickie and Dimma, who were less than enthusiastic but said they'd allow it if we couldn't do it anywhere else. Brickie had said, "What do you think you boys are? The United Nations?" and "Talk to your grandmother." Dimma had said, grudgingly, "It's a nice idea, but I expect you boys to plan it and see it through, *including cleaning up*. Don't forget that next week both your sister and your mother are coming for a visit, and that won't be a convenient time. And then there's your trip to Rehoboth with your father right before Labor Day, so plan accordingly."

I knew exactly when my mother was coming home and had been thinking how wonderful it would be if she came for the party. "But, Dimma, don't you think that it would be fun for Mama to be at the Fiesta? She loves parties!"

Dimma looked sad. "I don't think she's *up to* attending

parties yet, John. She's still very . . . tired. I think she only wants to spend time with you and Liz. Not with all the neighbors."

Without Elena, and with nothing else to do, we decided to mount our bikes and ride to our empty school to hunt for spiders there. This late in summer, they'd be cleaning and readying the building for the new year, and it was always weird and fun to sneak in when only the old deaf janitor, Mr. Offutt, was around. We'd sneaked in the year before, and on our teacher Mr. Sullivan's desk, we saw a list of students and their IQs. We didn't know what IQs were, but we were shocked to see that our refugee friend Gellert had an IQ of 135, when everybody else's scores were just over 100. We'd decided that IQs must have something to do with a student's height or athletic abilities.

We were pedaling down the lane when Beau and D.L. came out of their house and summoned us to play war. We didn't want to, but it was best not to rile the Shreve boys up. They carried their guns—we weren't sure if they were toys or actual pellet guns, but the Shreves were very realistic and could shoot dried black-eyed peas. They aimed them at us.

"Our mom just made cookies," said Beau. "We can have some after."

That made the offer slightly more enticing. "Okay," said Max. "But we can't play too long because we've got something to do."

"What? Looking for more *bugs*?" said D.L.

"Don't you guys even care that Russian spies dropped a spider bomb on Washington?" I countered.

Beau and D.L. looked at each other, skeptically amazed. "How do you know that?" Beau said.

"My grandfather told me. He found a poisonous one in his office."

"We'll ask our dad. He'll know if it's true. The FBI knows everything," D.L. said.

Then Beau addressed Ivan. "So *your* dad probably knows, too, since he's a Russian spy."

"He is not," Ivan said. "He's not even Russian."

"Oh, *sure,*" Beau sneered.

"And your aunt is, too," said D.L. It disturbed me to hear Elena dragged through the mud with Josef, and I knew it had to offend Ivan. "She's *definitely* a Commie and hangs around with them." They kept their guns trained on us—also disturbing.

"No she's not and no she doesn't," Ivan said, as forcefully as he could, his face flushed. "They left Russia to get *away* from Commies."

"That's just propaganda," I said to Beau, pretty sure Brickie's word meant *lies.*

D.L. looked me in the eye through his gun sight and said, "And *your* grandfather has a secret pen name for the stuff he writes: 'Guy Sims Fitch.'"

"What?" I sputtered. "No he doesn't!" What was D.L. talking about—could Mr. Shreve know things about Brickie that I didn't know?

"Are y'all gonna play, or not?" Beau demanded.

"Not if you keep saying stupid things to us," Max said.

"Okay," Beau said. They lowered the guns. "We take it back." Beau put one hand behind his back, no doubt crossing his fingers.

I sighed. "Which war and which battle?" I asked.

D.L. said, "We haven't played *Bridge on the River Kwai* in a while. Let's play that."

"Aww, rats," said Max, who knew he was going to have to be the pompous collaborator, Colonel Nicholson. Beau and D.L. liked to humiliate all of us, but especially Max.

"We should get Kees and Piet to play," Beau said. "Or we won't have anybody to play the chickenshit guy."

"Unh-unh!" I said. "The last time we played war with them we made Kees and Piet be Jews and we pretended their own Airstream was a gas chamber and locked them in. We were the American troops coming to liberate the camp, but the General caught us, and he went crazy and said if we did it again, he'd 'spank us blue as a mulberry.'" This was the moronic event that had ended our swimming privileges at the De Haans'.

"Wow!" said D.L., impressed. "Where were *we*? I bet the General has some special Nazi spanking things."

We dumped our bikes and began taking directions from D.L. and Beau. We made the infamous bridge with some planks and sawhorses hauled from the Shreves' shed, which was chock-full of webs, but Beau and D.L. wouldn't give us time to examine them. For the prison camp, we wrenched a few cinder blocks from under Mr. Shreve's fishing boat, causing it to list dangerously. We set the cinder blocks around a campfire made with sticks and trash. Beau lit it. I had to put on Beau's baseball cap with a washcloth hanging down the back of my neck because I was the evil Colonel Saito, which wasn't all bad because I'd get to abuse the heroic Allies, Joyce and Warden, played, naturally, by the Shreves.

The Ally soldiers, Beau, D.L., and Ivan, gathered around the campfire, smoking their stick cigarettes, talking tough and complaining about being forced to build the bridge by a bunch of Japs. Max, as the traitor Colonel Nicholson, ranted at them about how crappy their bridge was and insisted they build one that would be a monument to British military genius. After he left, the Allies talked about what an asshole he is, and spit a lot. Then I came over with a willow switch, hollering in fake Japanese, and whipped the three of them, which I did harder than necessary to Beau and D.L. I made the Allies stack and unstack cinder blocks, over and over in the broiling sun, until Beau took out a Rich's shoe box rattling with cherry bombs and put it under the bridge. The Allies pretended to go to sleep, whispering plans to kill Saito and blow up the bridge. Then I forced the Allies to march around in a circle. They began whistling the movie theme song and wouldn't stop, even though I was screaming at them. Then Beau stabbed me with a rubber knife and ran to light the shoe box as Ivan and D.L. yelled, "Here come tons of Japs on a train!" This was the point where D.L. always began reciting "The Charge of the Light Brigade," which had nothing to do with *Bridge on the River Kwai,* but D.L.

loved the *Little Rascals* episode where Alfalfa did it: "'Half a league, half a league / Half a league onward / All in the valley of death / Rode the six hundred.'" Then the cherry bombs caught and the train and bridge "blew up." Beau and D.L. kicked my and Max's dead bodies a few times, also harder than necessary. Ivan stood on top of the Shreves' mulch pile, shaking his head sadly, saying, "Madness! Madness!" We were all still for a moment in the cherry-bomb smoke, as if the movie credits were rolling.

The Shreves' back door opened and Mrs. Shreve shouted, "Good heavens, boweez! What were those explosions? What's that smoke?"

"Aww, Mama, it's just cherry bombs," said D.L., proudly surveying our tableau of destruction.

"I wish y'all would quit playin' with those annoyin' farcrackuhs! And please put all that stuff back where it came from. Deeyayall, put out that far. Your daddy will not 'preciate a burnt place on the lawn. *And* y'all have practice in thutty minutes." She smiled graciously at me and Max and Ivan, and held out a plate of cookies. "Would y'all boweez like some cookies? Theyuh peanut buttah."

We took some cookies and Ivan stepped up and told Mrs. Shreve, "We're going to have a Fabulous Family Fiesta for the neighborhood soon! It's a potluck. We'll let you know the details. We hope your whole family will attend." Max and I looked at each other, marveling that shy Ivan had become quite the Beaver Plan ambassador.

"Whah, how loveleh, boweez! And all the adults are invahted?"

"Yes, ma'am!" Ivan said. "It'll be in John's yard, and his grandparents and Elena and Max's mom and dad and *everybody* is coming!" I wondered how Ivan was so certain about *everybody*.

"Well, we will suhttenly be theah and will bring some refrayushments. We 'preciate the invitation."

We helped the Shreves put back the bridge junk, leaving them to deal with the fire and cinder blocks. The boat was obviously going to fall off its dry dock, and we didn't want to be blamed.

It seemed too late now to ride to Rosemary, and we were really hot after the campfire and warfare, so we went next door to Ivan's, hoping Elena had returned and we could make the posters. I was wondering about what D.L. had said about Brickie having a secret pen name, but it made no sense to me. Maybe I'd ask him.

Ivan's house was quiet, and Ivan said, "Good—nobody's home. We can watch TV." We yanked off our sweaty T-shirts and threw them on the floor, grateful for the dark coolness of Ivan's living room and the bananas Maria brought us, saying, "You eat—es good for you." Looking back, I've often thought that if not for Estelle and Maria, we boys might have been seriously undernourished. Except for Brickie at breakfast, nobody but those two ladies paid much attention to what we did or didn't eat.

Then Beatriz showed up, wearing sporty orange clam diggers and a matching top I'd never seen, saying, "Hi, guys!"

and sat down with us to watch TV. I handed her half of my banana, and we told her about the Fiesta. She jumped right in enthusiastically. "We should have dancing and entertainment! We could put on a skit!" Looking like a raven-haired Pippi Longstocking, she stretched out both braids excitedly and was full of ideas, most of which sounded lousy to Max because they involved dancing, singing, or costumes, but they sounded fun to me.

Ivan turned on the cartoon show *Clutch Cargo,* which Max thought was lousy, too. "You guys are such babies sometimes."

Beatriz said, "Max, Ivan is your host. Why are you so crabby?"

"He's not my *host,* he's my friend. I'm crabby because I don't want to talk about stupid skits and we had to play war with Beau and D.L. instead of hunting spiders."

Beatriz said sympathetically, "Okay, I get it. I *thought* I heard those dopey boys setting off cherry bombs."

She sat back, and we settled in, eating our bananas and enjoying the big oscillating fan and the way the cooling blue velvet of the sofa soaked up our sweat. Soon all of us, even Max, were absorbed with Clutch, flying around the world heroically.

Halfway through the episode, we heard flip-flopped feet coming down the stairs. I hoped it was Elena, but when Ivan stiffened, sat up, and left, saying he had to go to the bathroom, I knew Josef must be home. The flip-flopping continued down the hall to the kitchen. In a minute Ivan's dad came into the living room, wearing his bathrobe and carrying the newspaper.

He greeted us, smiling pleasantly, but a little creepily. "Hello, kids. You don't mind if I read the afternoon paper in here, do you? This is the coolest room in the house." Without waiting for an answer, he sat down, crossing one leg over the other, and opened his paper. "This spider business must be keeping you boys busy."

"Uh-huh," I said. Then, from the depths of his robe, I spied a rat's nest that looked more like fur than hair, with a bulbous purple *thing* peeking out from it. I giggled nervously, looking at Beatriz and Max, who only stared intently at the TV, Max red-faced. I pretended to be examining my banana.

Suddenly Ivan appeared outside the window, waving furiously for us to come outside. Max jabbed me with his elbow, and we rose, Max casually grabbing our shirts, while I signaled to Beatriz. "We've got to go now," Max said, and Beatriz said, "Bye!" as the three of us scooted for the front door.

On the porch I whispered, "Did you see *that*? He didn't know we could see his wiener!"

Max said, "Don't tell Ivan. He'll just be embarrassed."

"It's not a big deal," Beatriz added. "I see my brother's all the time. Once my cousin in Brazil tried to make me touch his."

I couldn't imagine this, although I tried to, and said, "Did you?"

"I just slapped it and said, 'Put that silly thing away!' "

Ivan waited in the hammock. His pale burr head was already sweaty again. "Did . . . did he bother you guys?" Ivan asked, looking worried. "I didn't think he was home."

"Nah," Max answered nonchalantly. "He was just reading in the paper about the spiders, trying to cool off." He smiled and Ivan relaxed.

From the De Haans' across the street came the annoying noise of fun in the pool. "I'm *roasting,*" I complained. "I sure wish we were in that pool."

"Pfft! Nazi soup!" Max spat. I thought about Chevy Chase Lake, a gigantic pool close by, but we couldn't go there because they didn't let Jews in.

"There's always *your* pool," Ivan said to me.

Earlier in the summer, after she thought we'd suffered enough following the Airstream incident with the De Haans, Dimma had gone to People's Hardware and gotten a blue plastic pool about two feet high and eight feet wide. We'd set it up in my backyard on the grass where a concrete pond had once been. The pond was filled in, but the fountain featuring a woman with a pitcher remained. Supposedly a woman had drowned herself in the concrete pond a long time ago. My mother loved the statue, and Sir Walter Scott's poem, and called her the Lady of the Lake. Stevenson, our old yardman, who ironically bore the same name as the 1956 presidential candidate, which hugely amused Estelle and Brickie, planted trailing petunias in the pitcher every spring. A few flowers still hung down, pink-and-purple-striped, but they were spent and ragged now. At first we boys had been happy enough with the pool, but we were bored with it by

July. Now the water was low and greenish, leaves and grass mowings floating on the surface, and its sides were slick with algae. "It looks pretty bad. Do you think there's any polio in there?" Ivan asked.

"Nah," I said. "We'll fill it up with new water and it will be okay."

We could see spider bodies on the bottom—none of the poisonous ones we were looking for—and mosquito larvae, wriggling like minuscule shrimp, but we didn't care. "Aw, what the hell?" I said, echoing every adult I'd ever heard in my entire life.

Beatriz left; she didn't have her bathing suit and said it was time for her to go home, and anyway, she added, it was "too icky," and we would probably get sick from being in it and miss the Fabulous Family Fiesta.

I dragged the hose over and threw it into the pool, and we jumped in in our shorts. The three of us thrashed and splashed, hollering even louder than usual, hoping Kees and Piet would hear us. Once the water became deeper, we made a whirlpool by running around and around as fast as we could. I pulled off the remaining petunias from the Lady of the Lake and tossed them into the water. Then we drifted around with the flowers in the current of the whirlpool, looking up at the softening sky, where swifts were circling with us, birds and boys thinking about food and roosting for the evening. Ivan said the swifts would be heading to South America for the winter. "They've probably been stuffing themselves with spiders for the trip."

Pretty soon, grown-up voices sounded around the

neighborhood, gathering their flocks for dinner and the night. Max and Ivan went home, and I went inside, calling out, "I'm ready for dinner!" as I let the back screen door slam behind me for emphasis, just in case anybody had forgotten I existed.

4

The next day we called a meeting—we liked to call our loitering "meetings"—on Ivan's front porch. Elena was finally available, but she hadn't emerged from her bedroom yet, so we went to the end of the walk and sat on the lowest step to wait. There were new spiderwebs on the old gate, and a few spiders in the corners of the steps, but we'd already examined those and knew them to be ordinary specimens—nothing we hadn't already caught.

We'd tried to get Beatriz to come out for the meeting, but she had ballet lessons. Too often it was either that, or piano, or confession or catechism, or she couldn't play because she had to help her mom with the cooking and cleaning, or with her poor sister, Zariya. We thought it was a drag that girls had so many dumb things they had to do all the time, and thank goodness we weren't girls.

We sat and waited, taking a few minutes for some thoughtful scratching. Then we pulled up pieces of the walk to see what we could find. Max and I set fire to some ants—the kind that often stung us. We didn't believe in burning ants who were on the job, although Ivan protested, saying, "Ants are *always* on the job."

Suddenly Max cried out, "Oh, no! Not the Advice Lady!" An old lady in a ratty hat struggled up the lane with a tiny dog. We called her the Advice Lady because she came around and gave out unsolicited advice and predictions: Don't play in puddles because you'll get polio; don't go without shoes because you could cut your feet and get lockjaw; don't fool with dead animals. She cowed us a bit; she was imposingly large at a time when most people were skinny. We'd been told to be nice to her because she was pitiful and mentally ill. When she reached us, she said, "I see you boys playing with fire! You'll burn yourselves to cinders! We have enough to worry about what with the spiders, and newcular war coming any day now!"

"Yes, ma'am," I said. She teetered on.

Max and I started in busting the tar-pops welling up on the hot street, exploding the liquid inside. Ivan seemed more quiet than usual and didn't join in.

"Brickie says he used to chew tar when he was a kid," I mused. "He said it was kind of like bubblegum, but not sweet."

"That's a big lie," Max said. "Why would you chew it, then?"

"I don't know." I wished I hadn't brought it up.

"Well, if it's true, why don't you try it?" Max said, swatting at me. With his big head and wide lips, he looked like Howdy Doody, and I said so, hoping to derail his challenge.

Ivan looked pensive. "In Mexico people chewed pieces of cactus."

Max grinned fiendishly. "Okay, so John can try some tar, and you can eat a piece of that cactus in your backyard?"

"Not that kind of cactus, I don't think," said Ivan.

"You're both chicken." Max flicked us with tar-pop juice. I pulled up a soft, warm blob of tar, rolled it into a ball, and popped it into my mouth. "It's like Turkish Taffy," I lied, trying to hold it in my cheek without actually chewing.

"Oh, *sure,*" Max said. Then, alarmed, he yelled, "You'll probably get lockjaw now. Or *yaws.* Spit it out!" We were horrified by yaws, a disease that caused big, open sores that we'd seen on people in Brickie's *National Geographic.* Almost as horrified as we were by the photos of floppy native bosoms and incomprehensible penis sheaths.

I spit out my tar cud, simultaneously throwing up some of the morning's Frosted Flakes.

Ivan shook his head. "The stuff they chewed in Mexico made everybody happy." He looked both wise and sad as he spoke.

The Goncharoffs' screen door slammed. There was Elena, resplendent in her kimono, holding up her hands with her Cuba libre and a sheaf of paper. "Darlings!" she called. "Here I am. Sorry to be late."

Checking the porch swing for bird shit and spiders, she reclined on her side as usual, but seemed a little stiff. We ran up the walk to her. "I have the paper for your posters right here. Ivan, I couldn't find your box of crayons. So you can use my fingernail polish, I guess." From her kimono sleeve she pulled some bottles of Revlon polish in brilliant colors and passed around the sheets of paper.

We accepted the paper and polish silently, not wanting to admit that when I'd gotten my new box of sixty-four Crayolas, we'd melted down Ivan's old box of forty-eight on his backyard grill, hoping to make one giant rainbow crayon, a waxen disaster that mercifully had not yet been discovered.

Elena took a sip from her drink, popped a Miltown, and settled the cocktail on the floor. She shrieked a little when a daddy longlegs ran up her hand, and I noticed a dark bruise on her wrist.

Max said, "Don't worry—they don't bite," and reached for her glass.

She slapped his arm. "No Cuba libre for you boys today. You have a serious job to do."

"Aww, rats," said Max.

"Well, what do we want to say on these posters? What was the name you came up with for your party?" I thought Elena was being unusually businesslike, not her typical cheerful self, and she wasn't bestowing her usual radiant smiles on us.

She handed each of us a couple sheets of paper and we spread ourselves out on the porch. We each picked out a fingernail polish color—I picked Sports Car, of course, and Max snatched a vivid orange called Tropical Punch. Ivan, our creative one, started right away making big pink letters in Cotton Candy: FABULOUS FAMILY FIESTA. "Fingernail polish is good because if it rains, the writing won't run," he opined. Max and I looked at his poster and copied him, although more sloppily.

"Okay, what's the rest of the information?" said Elena. "Like what day and what time will it be?"

We didn't know. "How about early evening? With a beautiful sunset, and it will be cooler?" Elena suggested.

Naturally we agreed. Everything became so simple with Elena in the picture.

"We have to have it before school starts," Ivan said. "And that's soon."

I added, "And I have to go to the beach with my dad before then."

Elena said, "So maybe Labor Day weekend would be good? That gives us a week or so to plan." She thought for a minute. "Let's do it Monday, September seventh. And that's *extra* nice because Labor Day is to celebrate all the working people."

We bent back to our posters and painted that in. "What time?" Ivan asked.

Elena said, "Oh, how about five o'clock? Cocktail hour." We added that. "And whose house will it be at?"

"My house!" I exclaimed.

"And that's okay with your grandparents?" asked Elena, raising an eyebrow.

"Sure it is. They love parties," I lied, remembering Dimma's peeved face. We wrote my address, 3512 CONNORS LANE, on the posters.

"And it's going to be potluck, right?"

"Yep," said Max. "We're bringing some kosher stuff from Hofberg's, and I hope some watermatoes."

I piped up. "Estelle and my grandmother will make some stuff, and I bet Maria will make those tiny tacos, right, Ivan?"

Ivan just said, "I guess so."

I added, "And then Beatriz is making stuff, and Mrs. Shreve . . ."

"And Tim did say he'd help us. There should be plenty to eat," Elena said.

We wrote POTLUCK across the posters.

"Beatriz wants to have entertainment," Max said scornfully.

"Very nice! What kind of entertainment?" Elena appreciated Beatriz's more sophisticated touches.

We looked at one another. "We don't know yet. But we'll think of something." I knew Beatriz would come up with an idea.

"Nothing dumb, like singing," Max added. "Just put ENTERTAINMENT."

Ivan left out the first *t* in *entertainment* and, since we were copying him, we did, too.

"What if it rains?" Max said. Everyone looked at me.

I knew my grandparents would *not* be okay with having the party inside our house, and I mumbled, "Umm . . ."

Elena said, "Well, just put RAIN CANCELS. And we'll cross our fingers."

We each made two posters and lounged around until they dried. Elena wanted us to be sure that we invited Gellert, even though he didn't live in our neighborhood. She thought it would cheer up him and his family, struggling with their immigration problems.

"Gellert always seems pretty cheerful to me," I said.

"Well, you boys haven't seen him since school let out," Elena said reprovingly, "so how would you know? You've never had him over to play this summer."

This was true. I tried to defend myself by saying "He's great at kickball, but he *eats paste* at school." This was a bizarre thing that some kids did, worse, in a way, than picking and eating buggers. "And he's kind of . . . dumb."

Elena said, "John, you know better than to say that! Gellert is actually very smart. He's just different, and he can't even speak English yet. I'm disappointed in you." Elena rarely got mad at us, and she was the last person in the world I wanted mad at me. Her frown was a punch to my gut.

"I'm sorry, Elena!" I said. "We *like* Gellert, don't we, Ivan?"

Ivan nodded slightly, looking away to make it clear that he didn't want to be associated with my ignorant faux pas.

Max shook his head and said, "Boy, you really put your dirty moron feet in your mouth."

Elena's mouth twitched, resisting a smile. "So we'll invite Gellert and his family and make sure he has a good time, right?"

"We will!" I vowed. Elena finally smiled, flooding me with relief.

The posters dried and did look wonderful.

We were ready to distribute them. Elena rose crookedly, as if something hurt, giving us each a light hug, not one of her robust ones, saying, "Good job, my darlings. I'm going to take a little nap." We gave her a poster for Gellert and rolled the rest up, stuffing the paper tubes into our back pockets.

We didn't want to post them too close to the Shepherd Street park, where the Bridge Hoods—teenaged boys a little older than Liz who lurked on the bridge with their transistor radios, smoking cigarettes and sniffing model-airplane glue—might notice a poster and think they could come to the Fiesta. We started down past the Friedmanns' and worked back up the lane, putting the last poster on the streetlight at the corner of Brookville Road, where the Montebiancos' house was. They looked grand, and we were proud of our work.

We collapsed on the ground to relax. We often loitered at this corner because it was great for spotting cars and license plates. A '58 Ford Country Squire passed on Brookville, and an Edsel. Eventually we spotted a new Chevy Impala with its cat-eye rear, and a two-tone Pontiac wagon about twenty feet long, and a beautiful Thunderbird with little portal windows. Ivan called an Alaska license plate—a first for us, since it was a new state. We chewed some long stems of grass that grew around the stop sign, then we made grass whistles—Max excelled at this. Holding his blade of grass loosely between his thumbs, he could create a low, rumbling, and gigantic fart sound, and this usually made us laugh as if we hadn't heard it ten thousand times. But Ivan didn't laugh this time, and I wondered why he seemed so subdued, and then I thought how Elena had been out of sorts, too, and remembered the bruise on her wrist.

"Hey, Ivan, is anything wrong?" I asked.

"I'm just tired." Then he said, "I couldn't sleep last night because of Josef and Elena fighting."

Max said, "But it's like with the Andersens; they always argue, right? So it's not a big deal?"

"I guess," he said, listlessly pulling at grass.

"What were they fighting about?" I asked.

"I'm not sure. She came home really late, and it was about that, and having so many dates. But then I heard him say something about taking her passport away, and something about a ring that was their grandmother's."

We were quiet for a minute. Then, not knowing what else to say, I told him, "The best thing to do is don't think about it. That's what I used to do when my mom and dad had fights."

"Grown-ups are always saying secret, scary things that kids have to listen to," Max reasoned. "Do what I do: Pretend that it's some stupid TV show, and in your mind change the channel and think about something else, like bosoms, or just turn it off. Sometimes I stick chewed Bazooka in my ears." He put an arm around Ivan and shook him gently.

"We should be hunting right now," I said to Ivan. "Finding some bad spiders would cheer you up."

"Yeah. I wish I had a tarantula for Josef." He smiled wanly. "I could put it in his cigar!"

"We need to look harder," Max said. He pointed across the lane at the Pond Lady's house. "*That's* where we need to look."

Just then two older ladies in a brown Frazer sedan rolled up the lane, the driver with her hand out signaling. They slowly pulled up at the stop sign and looked both ways about five times.

"Guys," Max said, determined to get a laugh out of Ivan, "watch this!" Ivan and I rose to our knees, knowing we'd better be prepared to run. Max took a few steps to the open car window and said, very meaningfully, into the face of the lady riding shotgun, *"Bosom."*

As we beat it down the lane we heard the driver lady shriek, "Did that boy say *bosom* to you?" We howled like wolves, even Ivan.

5

My mother and sister were scheduled to visit that weekend; my sister would stay until it was time for her to go to Holton-Arms for the new school year. As usual, on the rare occasions when my mother visited, I always hoped she would refuse to go back to the sanatorium, even though I'd been warned not to expect that; according to Brickie and Dimma, she was still sick.

Liz arrived first from Camp Furman, very tan, with dirt under her fingernails, which bore remnants of orange nail polish. I could see golden stubble on her legs, and her long red hair had been chopped off at the ears and stuck up in shocks and knots all over the top of her head. Kiss curls hooked on her cheeks stiffly, as if they'd been pasted there. Dimma was horrified.

"What on earth have you done to yourself?" she demanded.

"What?" Liz said with bogus innocence. "I learned how to tease it." She grinned. "Don't you like it, Dimma?"

"It's not appropriate for a girl your age, and we are going straight to Garfinckel's to have it repaired before your mother gets here. *If* it can be repaired." Dimma ran her fingers over Liz's head, smoothing the hanks that spiked up randomly. "What did you do—use an entire can of Aqua Net?"

"Mama won't care—she teases hers." My mother wore a short pompadour, clipped on the sides and high on top like the Everly Brothers', except that she dyed it platinum. At least it had still been that color when I last saw her.

I knew the truth about Liz's hair—that she had been brushing only the top of her long mane at camp, not underneath, and a tangled mass like an orange Brillo pad had developed, at which point she'd had to cut it all off. This had happened before, and I'd been the one to chop out the matted mess and smooth the remaining hair over the damage. Somehow this had gone undetected. "You look like Clarabell," I said.

"At least I don't have *scabs* on my head," she said, eyeing my ringworm. "I heard that enemas cure scabby heads."

This alarmed me because my grandmother believed enemas were good for everything. She often threatened me with them to scare me into better hygiene or behavior, but enemas had been administered a couple times. Dimma said, "That's enough, you two. His head is clearing up." It wasn't; it still itched viciously.

Dimma called Garfinckel's salon and told Liz to go take a shower, not a bath, and to wash her hair thoroughly with the Breck. Liz stomped upstairs to her room with her suitcase and slammed the door. In a minute, "A Big Hunk o' Love" was blaring. I followed Dimma into the kitchen. "She shaved her legs, too," I mentioned casually.

"Damn it." Dimma lit a Chesterfield. "She's headed straight for Florence Crittenton." Florence Crittenton was a place where girls had to go to have babies if they didn't have a husband, which I was a little confused about. Dimma went to ladies' lunches to help them. She said, "She'll end up like . . . God in heaven." She shook her head but didn't finish the sentence and began rinsing out ashtrays at the sink. Dimma used a lot of expressions with religious words in them, but we didn't go to church. I supposed that was why she said them—to make up for it. I wondered if she was saying that Liz would end up like God in heaven, but that made no sense, and in my opinion Liz was not destined for heaven.

Dimma and Liz returned later, Liz sporting a sleek pixie cut à la Audrey Hepburn in *Sabrina,* another of Elena's favorite films, and a red nose from crying.

"Now you look like Bozo," I said, running out of striking range. I was a little bit glad to have Liz home but didn't have any idea of how to show it. I felt like Max, who secretly liked Beatriz but tried to act as if he didn't. And I wished I could have my mother all to myself.

Liz yelled after me, "Why don't you go drink some Clorox with your dopey friends?" I'd once accidentally drunk some bleach that had been in a 7 Up bottle, and had to have my stomach pumped.

"Dear Lord, deliver us," Dimma said, shaking her head. "Can you two, for the sake of your mother, *please* try to get along?"

Brickie had already driven down to St. Elizabeths, my mother's hospital, which was just off Alabama Avenue in Southeast Washington. I badly wanted to go, especially since Brickie was taking Dimma's gleaming cream-colored Cadillac, but he said it wasn't a good idea. I thought he was worried, maybe, that I'd get TB or something, but couldn't I also get it from my mother? Another thing that made no sense to me, but I didn't press it.

They returned late that afternoon. For a second I didn't recognize my mother—I just saw a pretty, well-dressed lady being helped out of the car by Brickie. She was so thin and pale, practically the color of Brickie's tawny roses blooming in a bed next to the driveway, and normally in summer she was gorgeously tan. An inch or two of black roots showed bizarrely in her ice-colored hair. Then I noticed she was wearing a navy-blue shirtwaist that I liked, and her lipstick was her usual color, Revlon's Cherries in the Snow, so I felt better. Brickie, carrying her suitcase, announced happily, "Here's our girl!" Dimma rushed out the screen door to hug her, then held her at arm's length, telling her how wonderful she looked. At a loss for words, I ran to her, too, squeezing between my mother and Dimma, and wrapped myself around her.

"My baby!" she said, letting loose of Dimma and folding herself over me. "Oh, I missed you so much!" When we separated I saw tears in her gray eyes. "*You* look wonderful! Did you miss me?"

"No," I said, suddenly a little angry.

Dimma said, *"John."*

Mama just smiled. She hugged me again, planting little smooches all over my face, which I hoped would leave Cherries in the Snow smudges. I felt my anger melt away, and tears coming on, but I wasn't going to cry. "I'm much better now," she told me. "I'll be coming home for good soon, I promise."

Dimma said cheerfully, "Of course you will be, darling."

But I wanted her home for good *right now.* My mother ran into the house and up the stairs, calling my sister's name. I couldn't help myself and yelled after her, "Liz cut her hair! She has an ugly orange pinhead now!"

Brickie was in a great mood, for a change. He had always doted on my mother, his baby girl. I helped him clean the spider junk off the screened porch and we sat down to a long-awaited family dinner. Estelle had made her spectacular crab cakes—jumbo lumps of meat, one egg, a little mayo, a sleeve of crushed saltines, a pinch of Old Bay—along with corn fritters, green beans, and deviled eggs. The adults had cocktails and beer, and Liz and I were allowed to have a little beer served in Dimma's champagne coupes. Even my sister seemed happy, and my mother said she loved her hair, and that they would do their nails together tomorrow, and that Liz could help her touch up her roots. To me she promised a trip to Rock Creek Park to find some crayfish, and she wanted to see all my new spiders, and we could all go to the Moon Palace, my favorite Chinese restaurant, for dinner. Everything was so nice, *heartwarming,* actually, like we were on *Father Knows Best.* I was sad for a second, thinking about fathers knowing best, and mine being gone, but I'd see him soon enough for our annual beach trip, and I wasn't going to let that ruin the lovely moment. We ate and drank, engaging in pleasant small talk.

I told her about our plans for the Fiesta. "*Please* can you stay for it, Mama? It's going to be right here at our house!"

Liz smiled slyly at Dimma. "How'd *that* happen?"

"It's for a good cause," Dimma replied. "And I hope it might keep *some people* occupied, and out of trouble for a while. It's important to encourage children to have good causes—doesn't everybody think?"

"I think it sounds like a wonderful idea, John!" my mother said. "I'd love to come, but . . ." She patted her heart softly, or maybe she was indicating her lungs. "Dr. Overholser doesn't think I'm well enough to come home just yet." My own heart sank, even though I'd known better than to get my hopes up.

"You boys can always plan another Fiesta next summer," Brickie said. "*If* this party goes well," he added, a little pointedly.

"Or maybe at Christmas!" I said, hope springing eternal.

Liz said, "Well, *I'm* here now. I can help with the party." She scooped up a deviled egg.

"Umm . . . okay," I said, surprised, and not sure I wanted to share the glory for what I believed would be an epic success. So that Liz would know she couldn't be the boss, I added, "Elena has been helping us, too. And Beatriz." I took a sip of my beer, spirits buoyed.

"How is Elena?" my mother asked, touching Brickie's velvety roses on the table. "She sent me a sweet note at the hospital, saying she was going to look out for you while I was gone."

I was not going to spoil the mood by mentioning anything about Josef's increasingly disturbing behavior, so I concentrated on submerging my crab cake in the tartar sauce dish.

"Elena is a kind person," Dimma said.

"*Kind,* yes," Brickie said, passing the green beans around.

We chatted about the neighborhood, Liz's new school, spiders, Brickie's flowers. I was content. We were like a normal family.

Then the warm scenario was suddenly interrupted by a deep melodic voice calling from the street:

My knives, my knives, my knives are very sharp!
But my heart, my heart, my heart is so tender
Please bring me your knives,
I'll make them cut well!
Pretty ladies, here comes your tenderhearted vendor!

Brickie, in the midst of passing the platter of crab cakes, froze. Then he snorted, "Harry Belafonte needs to tally his bananas somewhere else." No one else said anything. "Another scrumptious crab cake, my dear?" he said pleasantly to my mother, who was looking down into her lap. Her roots stood out like a black scar on her scalp. She didn't answer Brickie, and he set the platter down. He reached over to my mother's lap and squeezed her hand. "It's important that you eat, sweetheart."

"The crab cakes are especially good tonight, aren't they?" Dimma said evenly. "Estelle was very happy that you girls would be coming home to enjoy them."

The singing continued. I knew it was James, the Jamaican knife-sharpener, coming around in his truck and summoning customers with his siren song. Max and Ivan and I liked James; he let us get in the truck and look at his knives, scissors, and tools while he sharpened them for Maria, Mrs. Friedmann, or my mother. All the ladies in the neighborhood liked him. He was handsome and cheerful, with a boisterous, musical laugh. Hearing his song now, I knew that something at our table had changed, but I had no idea what. My mother looked up at Brickie with a weak smile. "I think I *would* like more crab," she said.

Brickie placed a crusty cake on her plate. "You need to put some meat on your bones."

"Thank you, Daddy," my mother said. "Mama." She turned to Dimma. "Please be sure to tell Estelle how delicious everything is. I'm sorry I won't see her."

Not knowing what else to do, I reached across the table, grabbed a corn fritter, and stuffed it into my mouth. "Wow—that's *four,* Piggy," Liz said, her normal crankiness restored.

"That's enough of that," Brickie said in his most severe

voice. James's singing faded away into the evening. For a few minutes there was nothing but the clatter of porcelain and silver.

"Have you met any new people at the hospital, darling?" Dimma asked breezily.

"There are some nice people," my mother said. "But not many interesting ones." She pushed some food around on her plate. "Not anyone as interesting as Mr. Pound was, anyway." She looked profoundly saddened.

"Oh, I'll *bet* he was interesting," said Brickie, his voice brittle. "I'm sure he had a lot of interesting things to say about his buddy Mussolini."

Dimma said, *"John."*

I yelped, "Mussolini got shot and they hung him upside down in a gas station!" I was proud to have something to contribute to the conversation, but nobody seemed interested and everybody was either sad or mad.

"How come nobody wants to know if *I* met any nice people at camp?" Liz said.

My mother smiled. "Well, did you, sweetie?"

"No," she said sourly. "They're all square and stupid and smell like mildew."

My mother turned back to Brickie. "Daddy, that political mess is over now. Mr. Pound was just a harmless old man. He only talked about Italy and poetry with me. Dr. Overholser thought a lot of him, and didn't think he was . . . sick."

"Well, maybe they'll take a look at his brain like they did Mussolini's and they can figure out what the hell was wrong with him, then."

Dimma slapped the table hard and gave my grandfather a fierce look.

"Do people collect *brains*?" I said.

"Don't worry—nobody will be interested in yours, Scabby," Liz said, sneering. "They probably won't even be able to find it."

"John, will you get us a couple more beers?" Brickie asked.

I brought the beers, glad for a job. I bowed as I presented a bottle to my mother—"Your wish is my command, madame"—and the grown-ups laughed more than they needed to. My mother hadn't touched the crab cake but drank her beer thirstily. Then she said, quietly and as if she were far away, to no one but to everybody:

What thou lovest well remains,
the rest is dross
What thou lov'st well shall not be reft from thee
What thou lov'st well is thy true heritage

She smiled faintly. Dimma said, "That's lovely, dear. You remember that my mother knew Mr. Pound's mother in Philadelphia, don't you?"

I asked, "What's 'dross'?" Nobody answered.

After dinner, my mother said she was tired. She went around the table, kissing everybody good night, and went to bed. I went outside to find the boys and discuss what I'd heard, particularly about Mussolini and brains.

"Yeah," Max said. "They have his brain in a jar."

"But how can you tell if somebody is bad by looking at his brain?" I wondered aloud. "What does your brain have to do with TB?"

Max gave me a long look.

Ivan spoke up. "Maybe Mussolini got an earwig in there. That's what Maria says will happen if you don't wash your ears. They're called *tijeretas* in Mexico."

"Yeah," I said. "I heard one of Dimma's bridge ladies say that Italians and French people don't take baths."

Max asked, "Are earwigs the same as screwworms?"

"I don't think so," I said. "But Brickie told me that we should look out for screwworms. The government once dropped a planeload of something called Smear 62 in Florida or somewhere to get rid of them. Brickie said they eat flesh from open wounds."

"Gah!" said Max.

"Maybe he was just trying to scare you," Ivan said. "To make you quit fooling with spiders."

We thought about these things for a minute, since we weren't particular fans of baths, either, and we certainly had plenty of open wounds all the time. I changed the subject. "Did you see James?" I asked.

"He sharpened my knife," Ivan said, showing us. "For free!"

"He never comes around at dinnertime." Max paused for a second before adding, "Maybe he came to see your mom."

I was shocked by this remark, but I also felt a prick of

recognition. If it was true, it made sense of what had happened at dinner. I could only say, "My mom's TB is better and she's coming home for good soon."

"Maybe your mom had to go away because she liked James too much," Max said, nonchalantly poking a stick at a spider. "Not because of TB."

"*Your* mom likes James, too." I didn't want to continue the conversation. I was numb with the sudden realization that ever since my mother had left, I'd had suspicions about the sanatorium story, which had been the easiest thing to tell me and Liz, but I'd bought it willingly, not wanting to think otherwise. Since James was colored, I knew my mother couldn't like him *too much,* like a boyfriend. Could she? Maybe it was just one of the outrageous things Max often told us, like when he said that my sister was being sent to Holton-Arms because she was trying to "mate with boys," or that he *thought* he'd seen Elena making out with Dawn Allgood's boyfriend. Max wasn't trying to be mean; it was his way of cluing Ivan and me in to adult things, even if he didn't know if they were true. It couldn't be! I felt like a chump. Needing to change the subject, I said, "Let's get a jar for lightning bugs."

"Okay," Max said, punching my arm affectionately.

"I wish you guys wouldn't mash them," Ivan said with a sigh.

The sun was just about down, the very last of it dimming in the trees. The cooling air and descending dark flushed the lightning bugs from the lawns, and they rose, becoming blinking stars against the early-night sky. Unfortunately for some of them, Max and I would crush them on our bike tires so their iridescence would look cool as we rode up and down Connors Lane, a bat or two swooping overhead, until we were called in for the evening. Ivan would keep his lightning bugs in the jar by his bed, like a lantern, and let them go in the morning.

6

"We've done all the poster stuff," said Max, "Maria's going to make the cake, and Beatriz is doing the decorations, so we don't really have anything to do until the day of the party but look for spiders, right?"

"But we haven't figured out what the entertainment is going to be," Ivan said.

"I know what it's *not* going to be," Max said. "That's for sure."

"Beatriz will figure it out," I said.

We were outside, hunting and investigating—throwing worms and roly-polies into webs and watching the spiders scurry out to mummify and eat them. With Ivan's knife we dissected some egg sacs—lots of them were starting to appear. Max found an orange-and-black calico spider that looked like a ballerina in its web, and I snapped a picture with my Brownie camera. We had worked our way down to the Allgoods' house, where a yew was so covered with webs that, with its puffy red berries, it looked like a Christmas tree sprayed with canned flocking. We were so completely absorbed we didn't notice a bike approaching until it screeched to a halt in front of us, startling us.

"What do you morons think you're doing?" Slutcheon said.

"Nothing," Max said, covering the Big Chief tablet listing our spider inventory.

Holding my camera behind my back, I said, "We're just looking at spiders." Ivan scooched over behind me.

"Oh, yeah?" he said. "What kind? Oooh, daddy longlegs? How 'bout *this* spider?" He reached out and snapped his middle finger at my arm, delivering a powerful sting.

"Ow," I said, afraid to say anything else.

"I saw you guys are having a party," Slutcheon said with a smirk.

Max said, "It's just for people on our street."

"But we're buddies, right? I just might have to come." He laughed, his mouth reminding me of Foggy, the Andersens' dog.

Then Slutcheon pulled a cellophane cigarette-pack wrapper from his pocket. "I bet you don't have one of *these* spiders," he said. "I just caught it down at the park." In the wrapper we could see a black spider with a red marking on its stomach.

"A *black widow*!" Max cried. "How did you catch it?"

"That's for me to know and you to find out." He thrust the thing at us and we jumped back. Ivan let out a squeak.

"What are you gonna do with it?" I asked.

"Oh, let it bite somebody I don't like." He grinned

threateningly and put the black widow back in his pocket. "Maybe I'll bring it to your party. Hey, bend your arm," he said to Max. "I got a new trick for you." Slutcheon licked his palm, coating it with his disgusting saliva, and grabbed Max's arm, knocking the Big Chief tablet to the ground. Max bent his arm obediently, knowing it was better to submit and get it over with. Slutcheon began rubbing the crook of Max's elbow round and round, really fast, with his slobbery hand. After a minute, he stopped. The hairs on Max's elbow were knotted into tiny balls. "Now stretch out your arm."

"Yikes!" said Max, as the knots tugged painfully at his skin.

Slutcheon laughed. Having successfully tortured two of us, he turned his attention to Ivan. "Where's your sex-bomb aunt, Rusky?" He leered. "Isn't she usually *babysitting* you? You ever see her naked?" He sucked in some drool.

We said nothing.

"Her tits are huge, right?" he said. "She better stop bringing Commie refugees into my neighborhood, like that idiot Gellert. My dad's going to get rid of them. He's a big shot in the Immigration Service." He reached out to me. "Let me see that camera."

What could I do? I handed over my Brownie.

Slutcheon popped open my camera and yanked out the film, exposing every photo. Then he chucked the ruined film into the bushes. "This thing is a piece of shit. I just got a Polaroid." He handed the Brownie back, fumbling like he was going to drop it on the street. Which he did.

I couldn't speak. I could tell Brickie, who would call

Slutcheon's parents, but then the next time we saw him, he would just do something worse to us.

Just then a '53 black Oldsmobile 88 convertible came down the street and pulled up at the Allgoods', its radio blasting "Ooby Dooby." Leonardo, Dawn Allgood's older hood boyfriend, didn't usually have much to do with us, but he hopped out of his car without even opening the door and strode over. "What's going on here, squirts?" he said, really addressing Slutcheon. Leonardo picked up my Brownie and the Big Chief pad and gave them back to us.

"We're . . . uh . . . talking about spiders," Slutcheon mumbled.

"Really?" said Leonardo. "This doesn't look like a cheerful conversation to me." He stepped closer to Slutcheon and grabbed a fist full of his T-shirt. "*Just in case* you're messing with these guys," Leonardo growled, "don't do it again, punk." He let Slutcheon go with a shove, and our nemesis pedaled off furiously on his fancy Schwinn. At a safe distance, he yelled, his voice higher, like a girl's, "You'll all be sorry!"

"That kid's a loser," Leonardo said, and spit into the street. We agreed enthusiastically, and thanked him. "Where's your aunt?" he asked Ivan. Naturally he had a crush on Elena; they sometimes talked when Dawn wasn't around, and then there was Max's report that he'd seen them making out one night. We were shocked and skeptical when he'd described what sounded to us as if Elena had been *nursing* Leonardo, like Mary and baby Jesus, but Max had retorted, "That's not *nursing,* you dopes. *Gah!*" Maybe Dawn had gotten wind of it, and that might be why she hated Elena, and why I'd heard her yell at Leonardo, "That spy slut needs to go back to Russia, where she belongs." I didn't know what a slut was, but Max asked his older sister, who told him it was a "bad girl." But we were intrigued with Leonardo, "our local rebel without a cause," as Brickie referred to him, and we admired his cool car, dungarees, and greased-back ducktail with sideburns. He had a rockabilly band, Terry and the Pirates, who'd recently had a hit record.

Ivan told Leonardo he didn't know where Elena was, so Leonardo sauntered off, saying, "Yeah, well, tell her how I saved you guys, okay?" In the Allgoods' window, we could see Dawn and her blond combination ponytail-beehive peering out, and then she rapped on the glass impatiently, even though Leonardo was nearly to her door. We'd heard the story about the girl who had roaches in her beehive, and the Shreve boys swore they'd seen one crawl out of Dawn's hair.

"Man, look at this," I said. My Brownie had a crack on its side, and it rattled. "Do you think it'll still work?"

"My dad can fix it. He can fix anything." Max was rubbing the angry red spot on his arm. "We need to get back at that moron. We've *got* to find a spider that's at least as cool as his black widow and we've got to find it *now*." He slapped his leg with the Big Chief pad for emphasis.

"Yeah," Ivan said. "If we don't find one soon, all the spiders will be dead."

"I'm telling you guys," Max said. "Pond Lady's."

"Maybe we should think about it," I said.

"'Maybe we should think about it'!" Max echoed me with

a prissy voice. "Think about *this*!" He cocked a leg and cut a big one, one of his specialties. "I say we go for the Pond Lady's *tomorrow*."

Ivan said, "I do, too!"

I reluctantly agreed, remembering that I had to go to the beach with my dad the day after, so this might be my only chance.

"All for one and one for all!" Max put an arm around me and Ivan and we stumbled up the lane together, singing the only verse we knew of a Coasters song we liked to associate with ourselves:

Three cool cats, three cool cats
Parked on a corner in a beat-up car
Dividing up a nickel candy bar
Talking all about how sharp they are, these
Three cool cats

I couldn't resist asking Ivan, "*Have* you ever seen Elena naked?" I'd walked in on my sister once and she slapped me, even though it was accidental. Sort of. Also not very interesting, since she was about ten at the time.

Ivan said, "I saw her in her slip once, and I could see through it. It was scary! But she didn't care."

"My sister told me if I ever tried to peek at her she'd make earrings out of my nuts," Max said. Then, "I hope that black widow bites Slutcheon on his stupid butt and it rots off." He broke away from our embrace and pulled down the back of his shorts, mooning us, and started hopping down the lane, hands on his rear, crying, "Oh, no! My butt's rotting off! My butt's rotting off! I'm pooping everywhere!" Ivan and I doubled over, laughing at him.

Later that evening, as we were idly riding our bikes in circles, Beatriz appeared, coming toward us up the lane, her red hula hoop rotating expertly around her hips as she walked. "That's *amazing*!" Ivan cried. "How can you do that?" We boys weren't great hula-hoopers—maybe it was not having hips or butts? We could only hula hoop on our arms. Or get them hung up in trees; mine was actually on our roof. Beatriz stopped in front of us and kept swiveling, a big grin on her pretty face.

"Cool, man, cool!" Max didn't hand out a lot of compliments, especially to Beatriz, but that's how impressed he was.

Still hooping, Beatriz said, "Wait till you see my routine for the Fiesta!" We begged her to show us, but she wouldn't. "Surprises are more fun!" She stopped her hoop and we threw down our bikes by the Friedmanns' porch. Then she declared, "And I decided that for the entertainment you guys can do what you're already good at—Max can do his yo-yo tricks, Ivan will do magic tricks, and John can do archery! That way we don't have to worry about learning anything new!"

Max said, "Good. I'm sick of learning all the time." He was always cranky about having to go to Hebrew school *and* regular school.

We told Beatriz—we could trust her—about our miserable encounter with Slutcheon earlier and spelled out our plan to get into the Pond Lady's yard to find a revenge spider, although I was having serious reservations. She said, "I want to come, too!" She didn't care about catching spiders, but she also wanted to see the iron lung. "I like adventures and I never get to have any."

"How can you go with us?" Ivan asked. "You can't spend the night with boys."

"My mama and papa are going out tomorrow, and they'll be home late, and my brother just stays in my parents' room and talks on the phone all night."

We agreed to meet the next night at eleven o'clock, among the yews across the lane, where there wasn't a streetlight. "Everybody wear dark clothes!" I said, sucked into the excitement and proud that I'd thought of something.

Beatriz said, "I don't have any dark clothes. Except my school uniform."

Max said, "Well, wear that, Miss Priss."

"Okay," said Beatriz, concerned. "But I can't get it messed up."

"Anybody who's worried about messing up their clothes isn't ready for an adventure," Max scoffed.

"Well, I *am* ready, and I'm coming," she said defiantly, stomping a foot. "So there." I wondered why so many females, with the exception of Elena and my mother, seemed like our leopard-legged silver argiope, who would eat the males in her life if she felt so inclined.

7

The Pond Lady's yard on the corner was extremely overgrown—Dimma said that it wasn't overgrown; it was an *English* garden and was supposed to be *natural*—and her stagnant pond was irresistible to us and all manner of creatures. When we'd snuck in before, we managed to get some good frogs' eggs, which turned into tadpoles and then died. Ivan had fed them to Linda and Rudo, who gobbled them up like they were caviar. But we'd gotten caught and been cruelly punished by being separated for a weekend.

"You just want to see the iron lung," I said, still worrying.

"I. WANT. A. SPIDER!" Max shouted.

Surprisingly, Ivan yelled, "I. DO. TOO! We only got caught last time because there was a full moon," he said, always thinking. "And Josephine was still awake. It's cloudy today, and if we go really late this time, we can do it."

Max said, "I also wanna catch Peachy." Max was obsessed with the transparent frog in the pond.

We decided that we'd use our usual ploy to sneak out that night: The adults would be told that we were all spending the night at Max's house, which was easy to get in and out of because there was a good climbing maple outside the Friedmanns' upstairs bathroom window.

That night, the boys and I quietly played poker in Max's disheveled room to stay awake. We were prepared with a tiny penlight that would give us enough, but not too much, light. Brickie had all sorts of gadgets that he'd bring home from work. Sometimes he gave them to me, and other times, like this night, I lifted them from his bureau drawer.

A creaky hassock fan made enough noise to cover up any of ours. Brickie had taught me to gamble—he played a lot of cards with a group of friends at the Chevy Chase Club who called themselves the Jolly Boys. I taught Max and Ivan. We didn't play with money because we rarely had any, and instead used things from our collections. So far, Ivan had won the promise of my neon-green grasshopper and a scarab beetle from Max.

Just before eleven, when everyone in the house seemed to be asleep, we tiptoed to the bathroom, where the window was already open. We had to jimmy the screen out, but it wasn't a problem because the wood was soft with rot. I went first, then Ivan. Max came last in case someone caught us—he could think up the best lie. It was an easy climb down. We slunk to the yews across the lane. No Beatriz. Or so we thought—she was hiding, invisible in her uniform, and scared us to death when she whispered, "Hi, you guys!" Ivan and I pulled her up from her squatting position.

Max whispered, "I see London, I see France, I see someone's underpants."

Indignantly, Beatriz shot back, "These are *not* underpants. They're shorts." She lifted her skirt to show us pink shorts. Wiesie came prancing across the street and said loudly, "Wow." Wiesie was talkative and could often sound human.

"Shhh, Wiesie! Be quiet!" Beatriz petted her to placate her, but she said, "Wow," again. "Go home, Wiesie!"

"Let's go before someone sees us," Ivan said.

Walking single file, Max in the lead, we hugged the hedges until we passed the Shreves', and at the Montebiancos' we crossed the street to the edge of the Pond Lady's yard. There didn't appear to be any lights on in the house, but the vines were so thick it was hard to tell. Just then we heard "Wow" again. Wiesie had followed us. "Rats!" Max hissed at her. "Go home, you dumbbell!"

I said, "Forget it—she's not going to listen. *You* just keep quiet."

As we tunneled one by one through the Virginia creeper, ivy, and honeysuckle, Ivan whispered fearfully, "I hope there's no poison ivy in here," although he knew better than any of us that poison ivy was everywhere in the neighborhood. Webs clung to our faces. It was a noisy night: Frogs croaked in the pond, crickets chirped.

We emerged in the yard to see the lazy twinkle of lightning bugs and the blue light of a TV screen glowing through a curtained window; the rest of the house was dark. We crept to the azaleas under the window and peered in through a gap in the curtains. There was the iron lung, looking as metallically space-agey and weird as it had in *The Monolith Monsters:* a shiny contraption the size and shape of a coffin, with wires and a lighted control panel. "Wow! Look at it!" Beatriz breathed. The TV glared with the sign-off pattern, its blue light reflecting off the machine, making it appear *extra*-extraterrestrial, or like some kind of Frankenstein experiment. The Pond Lady appeared to be asleep—we could see only her white head sticking out from the top of the thing. Josephine was dozing in a rocking chair, her feet propped on a low stool.

"I told you guys it was cool!" I said.

"How do you think she goes to the bathroom?" Max whispered.

"Maybe she has to wear a giant diaper, like astronauts," said Ivan. "Or maybe there's some kind of drain underneath."

Once we'd gotten an eyeful of the iron lung, we moved silently toward the pond. Tall phlox and orange daylilies grew around it, and we could already see—and feel—more webs everywhere. I pulled out my penlight and snapped it on, keeping it low. Something plopped in the water and Beatriz squeaked. Wiesie, a striped shadow, prowled around and pounced on something, or nothing, and trotted off the way we'd come. A couple water striders were skating on the pond's surface, but they didn't interest us. Mosquitoes began buzzing in our ears and biting. I pointed the light around the decorative rocks. We saw a few ordinary spiders, and then some tiny eyes looked back at me—another wolf spider attempting to wrap up a luminous Hebrew moth. Then I shined the penlight on the webs draped on the tall daylilies, spotting a spider with a yellow ball on its back. "Marbled orb weaver!" I squealed, too loudly. I pulled a pill bottle from my pocket and trapped the orb weaver between the bottle and its cap. "Yay!" Beatriz whispered. I knew Ivan badly wanted to find something, but it was Max who spotted a six-spotted fishing spider next, and clapped it in his pill bottle.

Suddenly loud barking erupted from inside the Andersens', two doors down. "Foggy!" I cried. Lights came on in the Andersens' and the Pond Lady's. We looked at each other in alarm. My neck prickled.

"Run!" Max hissed. As we were scrambling back through the vines to the street, Josephine spat out from the back door, "James, if that you tryin' to creep up to this door, I told you we *done,* get on outta here!" Then, "If you *boys* be out there again, y'all better get gone fast 'fore I call your parents!"

"Help!" Ivan whispered urgently. "I'm stuck!" I turned to see Ivan struggling with a thick Virginia creeper vine around one leg. I quickly helped him wrestle it off, and we followed Beatriz and Max out of the thicket.

To avoid the lit-up houses, we beat it across the lane to Beatriz's, where she turned and blew us a fast kiss and hurriedly tiptoed into her house. The boys and I slunk behind the Shreves' and Goncharoffs' front hedges, stopping when we got to the dark spot across from the Friedmanns'.

"Do you think anyone saw us?" Ivan whispered, breathing heavily. The barking had stopped and the Andersens' and the Pond Lady's houses were black again. Max pointed to his house, and we dashed across the lane.

At the maple, we caught our breath and composed ourselves. "Made it!" Max breathed. "I think we're okay." There was Wiesie, waiting for us. I clicked on my light. At Wiesie's feet was Peachy, splayed out on his back like a tiny person. There were a few holes in him, and he was decidedly dead.

"Oh, no!" Ivan cried. "She *gigged* Peachy!"

"Wiesie! Why'd you do that! Bad kitty!" Max whispered angrily, shoving her with his foot. "We'll bury him in the morning. If Wiesie or Linda and Rudo don't eat him. *Or* we can dissect him."

There was movement on Ivan's porch across the street that caught our attention. A car—too dark to see the make—was parked in front of the house. We could see two figures in the shadowy recesses of the porch.

Ivan whispered, "It's Elena and her date. If she saw us, she won't tell."

The screen door slammed and suddenly there was Josef, speaking loudly and angrily in Ukrainian. One of the figures—a man, we could see now—stood up from the swing and came quickly down the walk, got into the car, and drove off. Josef's voice rose to a shout, and Elena answered, still in a normal voice, but excitedly. Then the two figures came together silently, in what seemed like a hug. We heard a loud slap, and a sharp gasp, and then the unmistakable sound of sobbing. It looked like Elena shoved Josef, and then she began coughing hard, making a hacking rasp between breaths. Josef shouted some more and the screen door slammed again. Elena stood alone, coughing and crying. Ivan pulled out his pocketknife. "I have to go help her!" he cried.

"You can't!" Max whispered urgently. "Then we'll get caught!"

"But it's her asthma!" Ivan said, beginning to cry. "And it sounded like he *hit* her!"

Max said, "She's got her inhaler and her pills, right? She'll be okay. Just wait a minute."

"What were they saying?" I asked. "Why was he so mad? Did Elena sit on The Throne?"

"He was yelling about her dates, like always. That she's making him look bad with her boyfriends and refugees," Ivan answered, pulling open his little knife. "She said he's just jealous, and he *is* bad—a khlyst."

I said, "What's a 'khlyst'?"

"I'm not sure. A creepy criminal, I think." He kept crying.

Max said, "*Jealous?* Why would he be jealous?"

Elena continued to fumble around on the porch. We waited. We heard the swing creak beneath her weight. After a few minutes the coughing stopped, and we heard only sniffling.

"See? She's better," I whispered to Ivan.

"Stop blubbering," Max said.

Ivan got quiet, and then so did Elena. We heard the screen door screech open and close as she disappeared. Some time passed, and the house went dark.

"She's okay, Ivan," I said. "It'll be okay. It's just another little fight." But we all knew it wasn't a *little* fight.

"Your dad reminds me of another Josef—Josef Mengele," said Max grimly. "Come on, we've got to get upstairs."

Ivan pointed the hand with the knife at the porch, crying in a strained voice, "I *hate* him! I wish he was dead!" Max and I looked at each other. This was the kind of thing he or I might say, but was shockingly out of character for Ivan. We'd heard the fighting before, but the hitting was new—at least to me and Max—and had shaken all of us.

One by one, we clambered up the maple and into the bathroom. Wiesie came up behind us. "We're not friends anymore, Wiesie," Max said. She licked her lips. Max put the screen back in place. We turned on the light and saw that we were covered all over with webs and greasy orange-daylily pollen: hair, arms and legs, shorts, and T-shirts.

"We look like we've been rolling in Cheetos," I said.

Peeling off our clothes, we all hopped in the shower and soaped up, trying to be quiet. Ivan was very subdued. I knew he was miserable about Elena, as well as sad about Peachy, and disappointed he hadn't caught anything. We dried off with one towel and hung it back neatly. Ivan and I put on some of Max's "clean" shorts from a pile of dirty clothes on the floor.

Max and I put our orange pill bottles on the windowsill, where we could see our new spiders, and he and I got in his bed. Ivan wanted to sleep on the floor, where the fan blew best, so he raked together a pallet from the dirty-clothes pile.

"Do you think we got away with it?" I asked sleepily. "Josephine said *James*. Why would James be in the Pond Lady's yard at night?"

"Jeez. You're such a dodo," said Max.

"Takes one to know one," I said back. But I really didn't want to think about James at all and regretted bringing it up. "Do you think our new spiders are better than Slutcheon's black widow?"

"'Course not," said Max. "The marbled orb weaver and the fishing spider are cool, but we *still* don't have a poisonous one for that creep."

"Yeah," Ivan said. "A spider that can really hurt somebody. Or at least rot somebody's wiener off." More rough talk from Mr. Tenderhearted. Max and I chuckled, but I was worried about Ivan.

Wiesie came in and Max told her, "You're *vanished* from my bed, Wiesie."

She went over to the pallet and stretched out alongside Ivan, who curled an arm around her. I was glad to see that. "You didn't *mean* to be bad, did you, Wiesie," Ivan said. "You probably thought you were bringing us a present." Lit by the streetlight, Ivan's sweet face was so clean and pale that I could see among his freckles the little circular scars that were vestiges of last summer, when he and I had had chicken pox. I thought about how much I loved Ivan, with only a drowsy twinge of guilt because I knew boys weren't supposed to love each other. I didn't feel wiggly about Ivan, but I would have done anything to protect him from what was soon to happen.

Within five minutes we were sound asleep, scratching our old crud and new mosquito bites, mumbling and dreaming who knows what.

I was confronted by Estelle early the next morning after eating most of a box of Frosted Flakes—dry. Brickie, the Colonel Saito of breakfast, had gone to work early.

When I came home from Max's at dawn, I'd stashed my pollen-and-web-covered T-shirt and shorts in the kitchen garbage, putting some other trash on top. I should have known better than to try to hide something from the ever-vigilant Estelle, but I hoped it might not be discovered until after my dad picked me up. "Who put these *perfeckly good* clothes in the trash?" she asked me, holding out the wad of clothes.

The first thing I could think of was "Those aren't mine."

"Then who they belong to? Your granddaddy?" Estelle demanded. "And what's this orange mess all over them?"

"I don't know," I said, trying to sound concerned. "Let me see them." I pretended to be examining them carefully. "Oh!" I said. "They *are* mine! I forgot—we had a Cheeto war."

"Umm-hmm," Estelle said. "John, you old enough to know better than to tell me lies. You take those out to the hose and squirt 'em off so they don't get that mess on the other things in the washer."

"O-*kay,*" I said grumpily. "Can't anyone have any fun around here?"

"That about *all* you have around here," she said. "You an' those boys need some chores to do, keep you outta trouble. Y'all nuthin' *but.*" Leaving the room, she turned. "You got all yo' things ready fo' your trip with yo' daddy?"

"I don't need anything but my bathing suit." Then, to placate her, I added, "And my toothbrush."

Estelle rolled her eyes. "You jus' be ready—he's comin' fo' y'all about noon."

I went out back and hosed off last night's clothes, leaving the wet wad in the sink.

Readjourning on Max's porch, we discussed the night. We weren't sure if Beatriz got caught, and we weren't positive that Josephine or the Andersens hadn't, or wouldn't, still report us. Hating to, I asked Ivan, "Is Elena okay?"

"She has a big bruise on her cheek," he said. "She told me that Rudo made her bang her face on the swing by accident."

I'd hoped the sound we'd heard the night before had been Elena smacking Joe, not the other way around. "Maybe she did?"

Ivan shook his head sadly. "She didn't see us, and I didn't tell her that we heard everything."

"What about your dad?" Max asked.

Ivan shrugged. "He went somewhere this morning. I hope he never comes back."

"Let's go get some candy," I said. "That'll make you feel better."

I borrowed a silver dollar from a stack Dimma kept in her dresser and Max was returning a bunch of Coke bottles with boring bottling locations on the bottoms for two cents each. It was only about nine o'clock, but we headed to Doc's, down on Brookville, to get some Zagnuts. They were Ivan's favorite, and I wanted to treat him. At the corner we stopped at Beatriz's house and shouted at her to come out, but she didn't. We hoped she wasn't being punished but was off doing some of her girly things.

At Doc's, we got a sack of candy and started back, eating our Zagnuts warily, keeping an eye out for an ambush by

Slutcheon. Back at my house on the brick steps, we polished off the candy and thought about more places we could hunt.

"We could go hunt around the basketball courts," Max offered. Famous high school basketball stars from all over Washington came there to play. Once we'd gone with the Shreve boys and saw Elgin Baylor play. Or at least Beau and D.L. *said* it was him. "Maybe the Russians put spiders at the courts to kill our basketball heroes," Max said.

"Russians don't care about our basketball heroes," I said.

"Sure they do! They just beat us in the world championships! But then they got disqualified because of some junk about China. They have a gigantic player named Krumins who's seven feet three inches and shoots free throws *underhand.*" Max clapped at some gnats in front of his face for emphasis.

Thinking of Sputnik, I said, "They're beating us in sports, too?" I'd have to run this by Brickie, but I knew he'd say that the Russians had cheated somehow. I heaved a sigh. "The world is the weirdest place on earth."

"Yeah, sometimes it seems like we're living on Pluto," said Ivan. "What about the park? We haven't hunted there yet, and that's where Slutcheon found his black widow."

"Unh-unh!" I said adamantly. "The Bridge Hoods will be there and might de-pants us." In addition to smoking, cussing at people, and getting high on glue, the Bridge Hoods were known for this kind of humiliation. Liz said they'd strip girls and de-pants boys. She knew a girl who'd been stripped.

Ivan tried again. "The castle?" Rossdhu Castle was actually the abandoned gatehouse to a demolished mansion with a disgusting brown lake. It was haunted, of course, and kids went there to scare themselves.

"I'm done with ponds," Max said.

"Well, I can't go hunting today anyway, 'cause my dad's picking me up in a while," I said. "You guys better not catch anything good without me." I was excited to be seeing my dad and going to the beach, but I didn't want to miss out on bagging a good spider.

Max said, "You think if we find something, we're going to say, 'Oh, it's okay, cool poisonous spider, we have to wait till John gets back to catch you'? 'Fraid not!"

I was miffed. "I'll only be gone *two days,* Max! If you do it, you won't be my best friends anymore!"

Ivan jumped up and said, "Stop! You guys are making my stomach hurt!" He ran over to a boxwood and threw up. "See?" he said. He pulled up his T-shirt to wipe his mouth. His scrawny white stomach heaved. "Guess I got too upset."

Max snorted. "Guess you got too full of Zagnuts."

Ivan did look a little green to me. "You look like *you're* from Pluto right now."

"I think I'm still tired from last night," Ivan said, his voice very weak. I was concerned, and I knew he didn't want to go home. But he and Max straggled off to their houses, wishing me goodbye—begrudgingly, in Max's case. He'd never been to the beach.

get there. We'd leave home in my mother's black-and-white '56 Ford Fairlane 500, traveling through downtown on Pennsylvania Avenue, then past endless tobacco fields and barns, arriving in fewer than two hours. Going to the ocean was fun, but there was more to do at the bay, where we had our cousins, whom we loved, to do stuff with. Our days were spent crabbing off the rocks or the shaky docks at Flag Harbor, poking at horseshoe crabs mating at the lagoon, foraging in the woods for turtles and snakes, and swimming if the dreaded sea nettles weren't evilly pulsing around in the water. Someone always got stung, causing painful red welts. On sandbars we'd dig buckets of soft-shell clams, which the grown-ups would soak and steam and eat dipped in butter—but they were too slimy for me and my cousins. My uncle had a sweet fourteen-foot runabout, the *Sarah Belle,* and we fished off it every day, catching rockfish and flounder if we were lucky, and creepy toadfish and blowfish if we weren't. Schools of breaking blues attracted terns and gulls, who dive-bombed around us. Best of all, at least for me, the bay's towering cliffs were striated with eons of fossils. Miocene shark teeth, seventeen million years old, washed down from the cliffs, eventually appearing at the waterline, waiting for us to find them. I had hundreds in my collection. Evenings we ate our fish or picked blue crabs and often played the quarter slot machines at Buehler's store—illegal for children, of course—and spent our winnings on BB Bats, Mary Janes, and Honeymoon ice cream. We all slept in the attic, telling lies and ghost stories, and doing rain dances if there was a storm, until we finally fell asleep. But since my mother had been gone, we hadn't been to the bay. My father didn't care for the bay; he said it was polluted. Also there weren't any bars there.

But Liz and I did love the ocean, too, and were always thrilled to spend time with our father. At the bay, I learned a lot of about natural history and wildlife, but at Rehoboth, I learned about a different kind of wild life. It was always a little . . . unsettling to me how loose the situation was down there. But everyone was nice to us, and Daddy always had a girlfriend who made sure we were fed and had Noxzema and Band-Aids. By evening everybody would be pretty smashed. My grandparents weren't particularly vigilant at home, and they certainly had plenty to drink every evening, but the Rehoboth trips had a crazy, anything-goes feeling. No safety nets. Now that Liz was basically a teenager, supposedly with some sense, we were left even more to our own devices. But Liz would often run off to the boardwalk, bribing or blackmailing me not to tell. I spent a good bit of time by myself, building card houses or digging up sand crabs on the beach while the men and their dates played records and cards, and drank and danced and smoked. Liz liked the dancing, I loved all the great records—the newest hit songs—but I didn't want to be forced to dance and look like a fool. Dancing with Elena or even Beatriz at the Fiesta would be different, I told myself. I just waited around, hoping for some time alone with my dad.

Later in the night, the partiers would pair off and make out in the porch hammock or go down to the beach. Sometimes a couple might still be lying there, wrapped in a blanket, when I got up at dawn to comb the beach. There wasn't much to find; there were no shark teeth like at the bay, mostly just whelk egg cases—those weird little black things that looked like dancing imps—but sometimes I'd find an unbroken sand dollar or a beautiful whelk shell, all purple and orange, the kind that you held to your ear to hear the ocean. Later in the morning, Daddy would swim with us, and that was my favorite part of every day.

At the appointed time, Dad pulled up in his convertible MG TD—it was British racing green, and looked like an oversize toy, and it amazed me that we could zip along the highway in it faster than all the boatlike cars of the day. Dimma waved from the front door, but Brickie made sure he wasn't around whenever Dad came by. Liz said Brickie was never going to be friendly again with our father, but it wasn't Daddy's fault. She was very attached to him, and it often seemed to me like she wanted to blame my mother for the divorce. I tried not to think about these things. And I tried *very hard* not to think about whether Liz knew about James—*if* what Max had said was true—and if that had something to do with Liz's simmering anger at my mother.

I ran to the MG with my grocery bag of necessities—my toothbrush, a beach towel, and an extra shirt. The babyish suitcase Dimma had given me now housed my rock and fossil collections. Daddy swooped me up. "Hey, pal! How's it going?" He kissed the top of my head and squeezed me. It wasn't like the relief I felt seeing my mother again, but I realized how much I'd missed him.

"I have my bathing suit under my clothes!" I yelled, jubilant.

My sister came primly down the walk in a yellow sundress, swinging her red suitcase, very ladylike. Her new hair was fixed perfectly. "Whoa!" Daddy said, putting me down. "Jean Seberg in *Bonjour Tristesse*! You look beautiful, darling."

"I missed you, Daddy!" she said, reaching up for a hug and a kiss. She reeked of her Muguet des Bois cologne, the only kind Dimma let her wear.

"I missed you, too, sweetheart. It's the one problem with living down at the beach—I can't see you as often as I'd like to." In reality, we had never seen him more than once a month even when he lived in town. It was tough for divorced fathers back then; they didn't have many rights regarding their children. But who knows—maybe that was the way they liked it. I hopped into the small space behind the front seats while Daddy opened the door for Liz, as if she were a real lady. "Here we go!"

As Liz and I were settling in, an old Buick turned in to the lane, the driver looking from side to side until he pulled up behind the MG and got out. "Whew. Just in time. Mr. Mannix?"

"Yes," Dad said, his happy expression changing.

The man drew a rolled-up sheaf of papers from his back pocket, cleared his throat, and said, "Sir, these are for you." He looked slightly embarrassed, and quickly got into his car and drove off.

My dad examined the papers. "Goddamn it! I can't believe this!"

Liz said, "What is it, Daddy? What's wrong?"

He went around the MG to the driver's side and got in, slamming the door hard. "Your mother's what's wrong," he said. "She's suing me!"

"Why would she do that?" Liz asked. I was scared that Daddy was so mad, and I didn't understand what was happening. "Who was that man?"

"That's a man who's hired to ruin people's lives." He cranked the car and we rode off. He didn't say anything else. We were down Connecticut past the basketball courts when Dad shouted over the noise of the wind and the engine, "I think your damn grandfather's behind this ambush. He'd *love* to see me behind bars." And then: "Never mind. You two forget about it."

We were silent. Daddy didn't look like he was going to forget about it, but at last he said, "Why don't we pick up some burgers and fries at Hot Shoppes for the ride?"

Nobody said anything. The possibility of Dad "behind bars" for whatever those papers were about stuck miserably in my head. I hoped the weekend wasn't going to be ruined now. It wasn't until we'd stopped at Connecticut Shoppes, and then made our way through downtown to Upper Marlboro, where we turned off, before Daddy seemed to cheer up. We played some road games—Ghost, and License Plates—and listened to the radio. Dad turned the music up really loud and we sang along, into the wind, bellowing out "Bony Moronie" and "Bye Bye Love" as we flew by cornfields and old farmhouses steepled with lightning rods. Then we had to slow way down as we rolled through a few sleepy towns—Denton, Bridgeville—whose cops were notorious for giving speeding tickets to Washington vacationers in fancy cars. The unpainted shingled houses were so pretty, I thought, trimmed in white, yards frothy with blue Bethany Beach hydrangeas.

When we arrived at the weathered cottage on Stockley Street, Liz and I went to the attic to settle ourselves—kids were always relegated to attics in those days. I tore off my clothes, ready for the beach, but waited for Liz because I wanted to interrogate her.

"Why is Mama suing Daddy? What *is* 'suing'?"

Liz was pulling on her bathing suit under her sundress, her back turned to me. "It means he did something wrong. I think it's about child support—you know—giving Mama money to help take care of us. I guess Brickie is trying to make him do it, since Mama's . . . sick."

"Well, why doesn't he do it?"

"He doesn't have a job right now, dummy. He *can't* pay it." She pulled the dress over her head, struggling so I couldn't peek, and hung it on a nail in the wall. The attic was spartan—there weren't any closets or furniture up there, only beds with naked striped-ticking mattresses.

Brickie was strict about things, but he wasn't *mean.* "Why doesn't Brickie like Dad anymore? Is Dad going to jail?"

"I don't know. Stop asking me so many questions. Why don't you ask your stupid Magic 8-Ball?" She grabbed our towels and started down the stairs. "Come on, John. And don't say anything about all that to anybody." People were always telling me things and then telling me not to think or talk about them.

We spent what was left of the afternoon on the beach, swimming and surf-riding with Dad and a few of his friends. It was a glorious day, brilliantly sunny and breezy—such a relief from the relentless heat and mugginess of the city. I was happy. I was with my father on a summer day at the beach. All was well. I buried the morning's unpleasantness as if it were a seashell in the sand.

That evening I sat on the cottage steps, waiting for dinner and for the sun to go down. I had a splinter in my foot from the unfinished floorboards in the attic but I wasn't telling because then Dad's girlfriend would root around with a needle and tweezers and alcohol and it would hurt worse than a shot. Dad was just inside on the screen porch, reading the paper and drinking a National Bohemian. His buddies were making a beer run to the Bottle & Cork at Dewey, the next town south. Dad's latest girlfriend, Carline, was in the kitchen with the other girlfriends making something for dinner, and Liz was helping. We liked Carline okay; she was nice and pretty—they were all pretty—but she couldn't hold a candle to my mother. And certainly not to Allison Hayes, who was Miss Washington, DC, when Daddy was engaged to her before he met my mom. She dumped him and went to Hollywood to become the 50 Foot Woman.

—

There I was, sandy and sunburned. My back and shoulders stung, but not too badly because Carline had put Noxzema on them, and Daddy had given me a National Bohemian with a few inches left in the bottom, which also helped. I could hear the rattling of Dad's *Evening Star* as he turned the pages.

"Dad!" I called through the screen. "Why aren't there any spiders here?"

"Don't know, pal. They're apparently only up in the city."

"Do you think that's because spies put them there?"

He laughed. "Where do you get this stuff? Your grandfather?"

"He said that Russians are good poisoners. There was a brown recluse in his office."

"I wish I'd thought of that!" he said—kidding, I chose to assume. "There are worse things to worry about with the Russians than spiders."

"I know! They have A-bombs, and Khrushchev said they're going to *bury* us. I get really scared whenever I hear a siren."

Daddy looked at me sympathetically and said, "I know, pal. We all do. But you're too young to be worrying about that crap—leave it to President Eisenhower; he's had lots of experience with Russians. Let's head up to the boardwalk later and play some Skee-Ball."

"Okay!" I said. I loved Skee-Ball, but you didn't win any money like you did playing slot machines. Maybe a useless stuffed animal. "Can we turn on the mosquito-zapper thing when it gets dark?"

"Sure, pal." Then he said, "Here's something that will interest you." He began reading an article in *The Star* about two very rare, scorpion-like creatures that had just been found at the Tune Inn on Capitol Hill. "They're called pirate vinegaroons and they're only supposed to live in the Southwest, and they're poisonous. They've taken them to the National Museum so they can study them."

This news electrified me. "For real? Is there a picture?"

"Nope. No photo. Maybe in the *Post* in the morning."

"Cool! I hope so!" I couldn't wait to report this to Ivan and Max when I got home. It was extremely important news. Maybe there were more vinegaroons around and we could catch one. That would be the jackpot.

Pretty soon the cottage was filled with people. It wasn't the kind of party I was used to at our house, which was mostly older, dressed-up people like Dimma and Brickie doing a lot more serious talking, drinking cocktails, and only a little dancing. This was more like *The Milt Grant Show,* with bare feet and beer—everybody bopping, most of the girls wearing short-shorts and the guys wearing Bermudas. Liz had put on her yellow sundress. Highball glasses and beer bottles were everywhere. I wanted the Fabulous Family Fiesta to be like this, except I wanted to be part of it, dancing with Beatriz or Elena. I tried to dance with Liz, who permitted my stumbling around for about three minutes, then said, "See? If you'd let me show you how to bop when I tried to, you wouldn't look like such an idiot now." This was true—she'd tried to teach me and Ivan, but Max had made fun of us and we stopped.

I watched from the screened porch hammock, occasionally slipping into the living room to sneak a sip from any unguarded beer or glass. A couple was arguing in a corner, and that interested me, so I listened for a minute, but it was boring—the guy was accused of "looking" at another girl. Somebody changed the record to "The Enchanted Sea" by the Islanders, an eerie instrumental that was popular that summer—all buoy bells, lapping waves, high-lonesome whistling, and mournful guitar. It reminded me of the bay, not the ocean, and made me feel even more dejected. The dancers came together tightly—even the fighters—to bear-hug to the slow music, swaying and kissing. I knew the hammock would shortly be prime real estate, but I wasn't giving it up.

Dad came out to the porch and said, "How's it going, pal? Don't you want to come in and dance?"

"I *tried* to," I whined, sorry for myself. "But Liz was mean to me. She's such a slut."

"What did you say?" my dad said, incredulous. "Do you know what that word means?"

"Max's sister said it means a *bad girl.*"

"It means worse than that. Don't say it, especially about your own sister, hear me?" He dragged on his Lucky Strike. "Jesus." Exhaling a dense plume of smoke, he said, "Hey—I want you to meet someone important. I'll bring him out here in a minute."

"Who is it?" Usually my dad's "important" friends were sports heroes or occasionally musicians, and he had one friend, Mr. Almy, who wrote books. *Dirty* books, Liz had told me. The sports heroes were okay because I could impress the Shreve boys, and Brickie was interested in hearing about the musicians, but I wanted to read Mr. Almy's books.

"It's a friend from Baltimore. He was the only guy who dropped both the Little Boy *and* Fat Man on Hiroshima and Nagasaki." He added, "But don't mention that to him, okay?"

My interest was piqued, but I didn't really understand why a guy who'd done something like ending World War II wouldn't want to talk about it. "Why not?"

"If you'd helped kill thousands of innocent people, even if it had to be done to stop a war, don't you think you might feel a little sad about it?"

"But, Dad, they were *Japs*."

"I know that, and they deserved it."

"Even little kids?" I said, changing tack.

Dad sighed. "The innocent people are what's called 'collateral damage.' It's terrible and sad, but it's what happens in wars. Just keep what I told you under your hat, okay, pal?"

Daddy came out with the guy, who didn't look very heroic to me, just a man somewhat older than my dad in shorts and a brightly flowered beach shirt. I got out of the hammock to be introduced to Lieutenant Jacob Beser and shook his hand like Brickie had taught me. "How ya doin', buddy?" he said. "Are you having a good time?" He did seem to have sad eyes, but maybe I only thought that because Dad had put *sad* in my head.

"I'm waiting for it to get dark so we can turn on the bug zapper," I politely replied. Dad and the guy laughed. "Are you still in the Army Air Force?" I asked. "Do you fly planes?" Maybe I could get *him* to bring up the Fat Man thing.

"Well, I was a radar specialist, not a pilot."

"Nothing can stop the Army Air Force!" I sang, and the lieutenant chuckled. "That's right!"

Emboldened by my entertainment skills, I asked, "So your job was to . . . fly along, and figure out where to go, and stuff?" My dad, standing behind Beser, gave me a warning look.

"Well, yeah, you could say that." He smiled indulgently. "Are you interested in military planes?"

"I like spies and *eshpionage,*" I said, trying to suppress the one thing I wanted to ask about, and not arouse Dad's temper, which I'd seen enough of on the ride down. I went on, "But I'm mostly interested in collecting spiders. I've trapped a few good ones."

Beser said, "That spider thing is nuts, isn't it? Do you think the Russians might be behind it?" He grinned.

This distracted me, and I excitedly said to my dad, "See, Dad? He thinks the same thing Brickie does about the Russians!"

Dad was grinning, too. "Maybe they *did* do it—who knows? Maybe we should send Lieutenant Beser's crew over there with some spiders for *them.*" They laughed.

"Yeah! That's a great idea!" I exclaimed. Then, as if from another boy inside me, came: "I'm sure glad you didn't drop those bombs on Japan." Brickie was always telling me to think *before I spoke,* and I *thought* I'd been thinking, but somehow in my excitement it just popped out of my mouth.

The lieutenant smiled but didn't reply. Tipping his bottle up, he glugged the last half of his beer. I was cringing inside.

My dad grabbed Beser by the arm. "C'mon, Jake, let's get you another beer and do some dancing." "Stagger Lee" was playing. Dad reached over and flipped on the bug zapper, then gave me a hard thwack on the head.

Lieutenant Beser said, "See you later, bud. Hope you zap thousands." He went through the screen door, and Daddy turned to me, drawing his index finger across his sunburnt throat.

We never made it to the boardwalk for Skee-Ball, because Dad either was having too much fun or was too pissed at me, or both. I was in disgrace, sulking outside. Someone brought me a plate of ribs to gnaw on. But the bug-zapping was a good show. I uncharacteristically helped a few decent specimens—a big Junebug and a dragonfly—avoid electrocution, and caught a great cecropia moth with my hands as it was resting on the silvery wood shingles. I let it go, maybe as moral chastisement of Lieutenant Beser, king of the zappers, whom I wanted to blame for my downfall. I hoped Dad would catch ringworm from thwacking me. And in my own misery, my thoughts turned to Ivan and Elena, and wondering whether things were okay with them.

I was up early the next morning, having slept in my bathing suit, and I was scarfing down stale potato chips, sipping from the brownish leftover cocktails and eating the cherries, shunning the clear drinks with olives. The cottage was silent except for the snores of a couple guys asleep on the sofas. The usual disheveled couple lay wound together in the hammock, so I sneaked out as quietly as I could. I knew Daddy and Liz were dead to the world and it would be forever before they were up. I was still a little mad at Dad and hoped to avoid him if he was still mad at *me.*

The day was going to be excellent; the morning haze was already burning off. I grabbed a red canvas raft and went down to the beach. Almost immediately I found a long, used rubber at the water's edge—a thing I'd never found at the "polluted" bay—and stashed it in my bathing suit pocket to show the boys back at home. We weren't exactly sure how rubbers worked but we enjoyed theorizing. A huge ship was moving quickly, way out, and I wondered where it was going. Baltimore? The Caribbean? Brazil? At home I'd tell Beatriz that I'd seen a handsome green-and-yellow ship going to Brazil, flying both American and Brazilian flags, people waving from the side. I guess the leftover cocktails had fueled my imagination. The waves were perfect for surf-riding—not too big but not too small. I wasn't allowed to go in the water alone, and the lifeguard wouldn't be on duty until later, but if I stayed close to shore, I reasoned, what could happen?

I grabbed my raft, dragging it through the surf until the water was waist-high. I climbed on and paddled out to where the waves were swelling before breaking. Steering the raft around to face the shore, I positioned it at the top of a swell, just under its crest, and the breaking wave rocketed me to shore. I was triumphant—usually Liz or Dad had to tow me out to catch a wave, but now I'd done it myself. I caught wave after wave. I wished my dad and Liz could see how well I was doing.

The big ship had disappeared, and it was just me and the sun and water and my competent surf moves; I imagined that I was the very cute James Darren in *Gidget,* another movie Elena had taken us to the Hiser to see. Could I possibly stand up on my taut little raft? I paddled out and easily got to my knees and waited for the next swell. As I rode down into a deep slough, ready to stand, I suddenly realized that the approaching wave was enormous; it seemed ten times the size of the others. I quickly flopped onto my stomach and tried desperately to paddle up over its crest, but it was too late. The huge wave broke over me, thundering down and tearing my raft away from me. I went under, squeezing my eyes shut and holding my breath, and was tumbled over and over, thrown against the rough bottom. I felt my bathing suit being ripped off. I struggled to right myself and reach air, but I was still being forced down. My breath gave out, and I sucked in water and sand. Finally my head broke the surface and I gasped raggedly for air. To my horror I found that I was not being pushed ashore but was now being dragged out into another slough, a wave looming over me. My feet searched frantically for the sandy bottom, and I started swimming shoreward, but the gigantic wave pounded me again. I felt like a pair of Keds in the washing machine—*slam, slam, slam.* The relentless waves kept coming—they became monsters hell-bent on destroying me. I inhaled more water, coughing desperately, and was terrified, knowing that I was in real trouble, alone and helpless. I fought with every bit of strength I had, but was exhausting myself. The turbulence wrenched my arms and legs—it was so painful I stopped flailing and tried to tuck into myself and float, but the water was far too rough. I felt tiny, a sand crab torn from the shore, at the mercy of the infinite ocean. I gave up, waiting with a weird calm for whatever came next.

I wasn't thinking that I was dying—I wasn't thinking at all—but understood that I was *losing.* Faces of people I loved appeared to me, most vividly my mother, and her voice, reciting the poem: "What thou lov'st well shall not be reft from you." Then my dad's face appeared, larger and more distinct than the others. I was lifted up from the water—was I flying?—my back being thumped. I began choking. My eyes opened to see that it was my actual father, who hoisted me to his chest and held me tightly, rushing me out of the waves. While sloshing wildly through the breaking surf, Daddy threw me upside down and kept punching me on the back with his fist. I coughed up seawater, sand, potato chips, bourbon, and cherries, which ran down Daddy's legs into the water. I breathed, and he righted me, saying, into my face, "I got you. I got you, pal. Take it easy." I was naked, clinging like a chimp to my father. *My father.* I buried my face in his freckled pink neck, tasting its saltiness and coughing. As we reached the sand, I looked out to sea and could just make out my red raft, which seemed as far away as the ship had been. Liz stood on the beach crying. I didn't cry. Daddy wrapped me in a towel and carried me in his arms back to the cottage.

Liz hadn't teased me—yet—about what had happened, especially about losing my bathing suit, which I took to be a measure of how scared she'd been. She didn't even tell our grandparents, because it would have gotten Daddy in trouble. Dad had immediately told Dimma that I'd "had an accident." I guess he'd had to tell Dimma *something* because of what I was calling my "open wounds," but he'd simply explained, "John got a little scragged by a wave." Dimma seemed concerned, but thank God hadn't wanted to give me an enema and had only said, "Well, I'm sure he was doing something he wasn't supposed to." Daddy had let it go at that.

"If you're still coughing tomorrow, we're going to see Dr. Spire," Dimma said that evening. Dr. Spire meant shots, and maybe taking off my pants. I whined, struggling to suppress a cough, "No, Dimma! If there's a sand crab in my lungs he's dead by now."

"Never mind," she said sternly. "And either you let your grandfather get that splinter out of your foot now, or Dr. Spire can do it tomorrow. It looks infected."

"No, it's not! It's better and I can feel it coming out."

"You heard me," she said, and gave me a goodbye kiss.

"Thanks a lot, dear," Brickie said to her sarcastically. He looked at me and shook his head.

Dimma was going out for the evening—playing bridge, I guess, although I noticed she'd forgotten her score pad, which she never was without. She looked pretty in her new dress from Claire Dratch, a pale-aqua shirtwaist with small bronze polka dots, which seemed dressed up for bridge.

I don't know where Liz was—spending the night with a friend, supposedly, but she most likely had sneaked up to the Youth Center on Wisconsin to hear a band, or make out.

Brickie and I were having what he called "Bachelor Night," which meant that he'd make hamburgers and hash browns for dinner and we'd eat Honeymoon ice cream and watch TV together.

Brickie loved *Peter Gunn* because Gunn was a private detective who dressed cool and had a lounge-singer girlfriend and sometimes in the lounge there were real-life famous jazz musicians playing. I would rather have been watching *Sugarfoot* or *Bat Masterson,* or Brickie's other favorite show, *Behind Closed Doors,* which was based on the experiences of an actual U.S. naval intelligence officer who caught spies and busted up Russian plots, but for some reason it had gone off the air. Brickie, who knew the guy the show was based on, said either he'd run out of stories or the Russians had gotten him. But I let Brickie have his way, and if we watched *Peter Gunn* I'd get to stay up later.

"Okay, mister," Brickie said. "Let's get this operation over with before our show comes on."

"Rats, Brickie. I don't want to!"

"I don't want to, either, but what *we* want doesn't particularly matter. What your grandmother wants is law. As you ought to know. Give me that foot."

I stuck out my leg across his lap. "This is going to hurt me more than it hurts you," he said, putting on his reading glasses.

"That's such a giant lie!"

Brickie chuckled, unwrapping a clean towel in which Dimma had left the instruments of torture: a gleaming sewing needle and tweezers, cotton balls, and peroxide. "All you have to do is hold still, and I'll have it out in a second."

"Oh, *sure.*" I was trying not to cry.

Picking up Dimma's sterling table lighter, Brickie clicked it and held the needle in the flame to sterilize it. Then he unceremoniously poked the needle into my foot, and, of course, I shrieked and tried to jerk away. He had a good grip on me, though. "Could you try being just a little stoic?"

"What's that?" I whimpered.

"*Stoic* means you try to endure things that hurt and don't let them bother you." He dug around and squeezed the inflamed spot, drawing pus and blood.

"Ow! Ow! Ow!" I yelled. "*Stoic* sounds like *stupid* to me." I was about to say that he should be sorry for torturing me since I'd nearly died, but I thought better of it. I tried to concentrate on the top of Brickie's head, where his faded red hair had thinned so I could see the tender geography of his scalp, the moles and age spots, which gave me a pang. Even though at the moment I was angry with him for tormenting me, I would miss him if I were dead. It also crossed my mind to ask about why he was being mean to my father, suing him—I was thinking about jail and wondering if Daddy had the money to avoid it—but I thought better of that, too.

Brickie traded the needle for the tweezers and plucked the splinter out, holding it up triumphantly. "Mission accomplished!" Then he rubbed some peroxide in the wound—hard—with a cotton ball, causing another "Ow!"

and stuck a Band-Aid on it. "Dr. Dimma was right—it was infected. See—that took all of four minutes, you big baby." He laughed and patted my leg.

"Hmpf. The next time you get something cut open I'm going to laugh at *you*. Like your hemorrhoids."

"I would not advise that," Brickie said. "Now let's have some Honeymoon and watch the show." He went to the kitchen to get our ice cream and I used the time to soak a new cotton ball in peroxide and stroke it across my hair, thinking I might achieve a blondish Troy Donahue look. Elena would love it. I wished I could dye it the platinum color of my mother's hair, but that would mean smearing revolting blue glop that smelled like rotten eggs on my head.

Brickie returned with two big bowls. "Are you sure *Peter Gunn* won't be too frightening for you?" he teased.

"The only thing I'm frightened of right now is *you*," I said. He gave an ice-creamy chortle and we waited for *Peter Gunn* to begin. "I hope you managed to have some fun at the beach before you were so tragically wounded."

I thought, *If you only knew,* but said, "I met one of the guys who dropped the bombs on Japan."

"Really." He seemed interested. "Was it your father's friend from Baltimore?"

"Umm . . . Lieutenant Beser?"

"He's a hero. That's nice that you got to meet him."

"I don't get it about heroes. He didn't *save* anybody."

"Well, what he did put an end to the war, so he saved a lot more Americans from dying."

Just what my father had said. I thought about our war reenactments, like the cruel debacle with Kees and Piet and their Airstream. "*We* like war, but is playing it the same as guys having real wars? I mean, why do people keep having them?"

"You boys playing war is different—you're just children, and you like winning, like a baseball game. There are real wars because people have to protect what's important to them. And war is terrible; no one 'likes' it."

It didn't seem so different to me. "But America likes winning, too."

Brickie shook his head. "There's always going to be a lunatic around to start something, like Hitler, and something has to be done about it. Americans don't *start* wars, we *end* them."

"Why can't we just do like the Romans? You just put the presidents and kings and dictators in a ring, like gladiators, and let them fight it out. Whoever doesn't die wins, and all the regular people don't have to get killed."

"It just doesn't work that way. But philosophically, it's a good idea." I was glad to get some credit for a change.

Brickie plucked at a nostril, and, feeling that I now had the moral high ground, I said, "Stop picking your nose, Brickie."

"I am not picking my nose, John. I had an itch. And you're certainly not one to talk about nose-picking."

I still had my doubts and persisted with my interrogation. "But it seems like people *do* like war. Beau Shreve said his dad said that American spies knew that Pearl Harbor was going to happen, but nobody tried to stop it because we *wanted* to get in the war."

"Yes, I know that theory. It's very complicated, son. You'll understand when you're older."

I hated that answer, which I often got from my grandparents. "Why do we make such a big deal about Russian spies? Don't we spy on everybody, too?"

Brickie sighed. "Why don't you eat your ice cream? I'm *spying* on your bowl right now, and you're letting it melt."

"I *like* it all melty, like a milkshake. That's the best way to eat it." I stirred it around and stirred around some thoughts in my head. "So if you think I should eat my ice cream before it melts because that's the best way to do it, and I don't believe that, it's like Commies and Americans—we have to fight about whose way is the best, and make everybody do it the same?"

"Good God, son. How many Cokes did your grandmother let you have today?"

"Three," I said. "It would have been four but Estelle took one away from me. Do you know any spies? Do you know somebody named Guy Fitch?"

This seemed to take Brickie aback, but he said, "How do you know that name? No, I don't know him. And nobody knows who spies are because they have to keep their jobs secret."

"Maari Andersen thinks you're a spy." This was a lie; it had been the Shreve boys who'd said it, but I knew they'd beat the crap out of me if I told on them and got them in trouble.

Brickie laughed. "Well, consider the source of that ridiculous idea. Maari needs to be worrying about *her* . . . *unusual* family, not yours. I think you know what I mean."

"Yeah. I'm glad you're not a queer."

"We don't say that word around the Andersens. Or anyone else, for that matter."

I wondered why all these words existed if people weren't supposed to use them, but instead asked, "Do you think I'll ever be in a war?"

"I certainly hope not. But you never know. Things are always happening in the world. It's possible that in ten years or so, when you're old enough to be in the military, it could happen."

I was mildly alarmed. "Where would it be?" Talking about and playing war were okay, but the idea of actually being in one startled me.

"Well, as I'm sure you're aware, Cuba's a mess—the Communists have taken over there. And Communism is spreading everywhere, and needs to be stopped. We didn't fight a world war to give people freedom just to have it taken away again. We got Korea under control. Just this summer, some American military advisers were killed in an Asian country called Vietnam, and it's a problem area. Not to mention Russia, of course, which is the cause of all the Communism, and is a terrible threat to us." He looked away for a moment, then turned back to me. "And yes, you'd probably have to go. When your country goes to war, it's your duty to defend it. And, since you apparently *like* war, that should be fine with you, right?" He raised his beetley brows, looking me in the eye.

"I might change my mind. And I'm not going if Liz doesn't have to go, too. Why don't girls have to fight? And I'm not going without Ivan and Max, either."

"Jesus, you are hopped up. Can this discussion be over, do you think? The show's about to start." He put his feet up on the coffee table and retrieved the remains of his pre-dinner Scotch, offering me a sip. I took a big one, shuddering from its burn. Picking up my bowl, I drank my ice cream, melted to perfection, to quench the heat of the Scotch and keep from coughing. Brickie said, disapprovingly, "Where did you grow up? China?"

I coughed, burped, and grinned. "Uranus."

"Very funny. I don't want you to say another word while we're watching the show. Think you can do that? Or do I have to go get the duct tape from the kitchen drawer?"

It seemed to me that our conversation had just gone in a big circle, but I didn't say that. I said, "That's playing Quaker. Ivan can go the longest without talking. If you duct-tape my mouth, stuff will have to come out of my nose when I cough."

"Those are your last words, my friend."

The menacing, noir Henry Mancini theme cranked up, and we settled in. The episode, "Skin Deep," was a summer rerun, but that didn't bother Brickie. "This is a good one!" he said. Peter Gunn was worrying about a rich lady who worked in a flower shop and had been clubbed to death with a fireplace poker. I had some questions but kept my mouth shut. Gunn showed up at a bar. Then Brickie said excitedly, "Listen to this, John! That's Laurindo Almeida, one of the greatest guitar players in the world!" We listened. It sounded pretty good, like the music that the Montebiancos listened to. "Wasn't that wonderful?" Brickie said. I wanted to impress him and say that Beatriz told me that that kind of music was Brazilian and called *samba,* but I covered my mouth and made muffled sounds. "Oh, right. You're under a gag order. Good man." We watched some more stuff—I don't know what—and I began to feel sleepy. Pretty soon I was nestled against my grandfather with his arm around me, sound asleep.

I felt better the next day, and after lunch I was finally liberated by successfully convincing Dimma that my cough was gone, although it wasn't. She was glad about the splinter, but Brickie took all the credit, and she made me wear a sock on my bad foot. I couldn't wait to get to the boys with all my news about drowning, and vinegaroons.

I limped over to the Goncharoffs', my bones still a little achy and my foot sore from Brickie's surgery. Ivan and Max sat on the steps at the street. Max had been dragging a magnet tied to a string, picking up a pile of iron filings. Ivan was polishing a dime with a ball of mercury from a thermometer he'd broken on purpose. I was glad he didn't seem sick anymore.

Ivan shouted, "YAY! You're back! We didn't catch anything while you were gone!" as I crossed the lane to them. Then, seeing my battered body, mapped with mercurochrome, and my socked foot, he cried, "Are you okay?"

"Man, what happened?" asked Max. "That mercurochrome looks like blood! That's so cool." I was shirtless because my scabs stuck to T-shirts and hurt.

"I *drownded*," I said, delighted to tell my tale. "It wasn't cool at all. It was *so scary*. I think I was *dead* for a little bit." I told the whole story, leaving out only the part about losing my bathing suit.

Ivan looked horrified. "I'm really glad you didn't die for good."

Max was less moved. "Did your life pass before your eyes?" he wanted to know. "Did you see God, or anybody like that?"

"I saw people. My family, and you guys, I think." I thought for a minute. "It was kind of like when we pull the legs off Japanese beetles and they can't do anything, maybe?"

"That's why we shouldn't do that stuff," Ivan said. He had a point.

Remembering my other big news, I said excitedly, "But you guys, *get this*! My dad saw an article in the paper about some rare scorpion things they found downtown. They're called *pirate vinegaroons*. There wasn't a picture, but there might be one in yesterday's paper. Brickie took his to work before I could see."

"Josef probably still has it," Ivan said, hopping up. "I'll

find it." He ran up the walk into the house and came right back with the Sunday *Post*. "Got it!"

Max and I huddled around Ivan, who found the vinegaroon article on the second page. There was a photograph of one of the vinegaroons, and it was shocking. The thing looked like a scorpion, but seemed more sinister because it was very dark, nearly black, had a long tail like a whip, and fangs, and was huge. It was pictured next to a beer bottle at the Tune Inn, at 331 Pennsylvania Avenue on Capitol Hill, where two of the creatures were found, and was nearly as long as the bottle was wide. Its appearance was terrifying.

"Gah!" said Max. "It looks like the giant ant in *Them!*" This was another of our favorite nuclear horror movies. "Is it poisonous?"

"Let me read what it says," said Ivan. " 'The pirate vinegaroon exists exclusively in the arid southwestern U.S., Mexico, Central and South America, and on some Caribbean islands, but even in those regions it is rare. There is no record of them having been found in any other areas of the United States. According to Professor Marion R. Smith of the Department of Agriculture' . . . blah blah blah." Ivan scanned the article for more juicy stuff. " 'The pirate vinegaroon is a member of the' "—here Ivan had to sound it out—" 'Ur . . . op . . . y . . . gi order, known as whip scorpions, most of which possess stingers like the common American scorpion they are related to. But the pirate vinegaroon has both a venomous bite and a whip-like tail that secretes a harmful spray, as well as powerful pincers to catch its prey—insects and small vertebrates.' "

Ivan stopped reading for a minute and we looked at one another, wide-eyed. "Man!" said Max. "It eats *animals*!"

"A whip *and* fangs!" I said. "Read some more."

Ivan resumed. " 'In order to catch its prey, the pirate vinegaroon will dart out, secure the prey with its pincers, bite it with its venomous fangs, and then eat it live. It is thought that the whiptail's acid spray is used defensively against animals who try to attack it. The spray smells strongly of vinegar, hence the creature's name, and can sicken or blind humans temporarily. The pirate vinegaroon is reclusive, making its home in burrows, under rocks, or in wood piles, and is nocturnal, and that fact, along with its rarity, is why few human deaths from its sting have been reported in the U.S.; only about five or six are known. It is very aggressive, unlike other related scorpions who avoid pro . . . vo . . . ca . . . tion, and if disturbed or exposed, the pirate vinegaroon will attack. Pirate vinegaroons can live as long as four to seven years, although the female often dies from starvation and stress after giving birth and carrying up to thirty of her young on her back. The two discovered at the Tune Inn are a male and a pregnant female. Metropolitan Police suggest using extreme caution if unusual insects or spiders are encountered, and ask citizens to contact them in this event.'

"It says no one has figured out why all the spiders and the vinegaroons are in Washington," Ivan said.

I said, "Maybe it *is* spies doing it. Maybe they *did* drop a spider bomb on us."

Max's eyes were lit with inspiration, fixated on his

obsession. "'Sicken or blind'! Boy, what I wouldn't give to let that thing loose on Slutcheon!"

Ivan was quiet, thinking. "They said the two vinegaroons they caught are on exhibit at the National Museum, in the Zoology Department. We could . . . go see them."

"Pfft!" scoffed Max. "We need to *catch* one, not *look* at it!"

I said, "Where is it dry, with some rocks, around here?"

Ivan said, "There aren't any rocks at the Tune Inn! A vinegaroon might be anywhere."

"And now we know *exactly* where two are," Max said very seriously.

Ivan and I looked at each other. Then we looked at Max. "I know what you're thinking, Max," I said. "No way! You're *nuts*."

"But maybe it's *not* so nuts," Ivan said. I was about to reason with them when Elena came out onto the porch, swelling our hearts. Max quickly scooped his iron filings into his orange pill bottle and Ivan put his mercury ball and dime into his green one and we ran to the porch to join her. Or *they* ran—I gimped along more pitifully than was necessary, hoping Elena would notice.

She seemed her normal self, although pale bruises were still visible on her wrist, and under her makeup, but faded to yellow.

She brushed some webs off her shoulders, saying, "Ugh! I'm so sick of these horrible things." Then she flopped on her swing, and, noticing me, exclaimed, "Darling! What's happened to you?" Elena opened her arms and I fell in, not caring that it hurt, coughing theatrically. She pushed me away after a quick hug so she could survey the damage more closely. "My poor baby! Did you fall off your bike?"

Max, jealous, said, "That's not blood, it's mercurochrome. It's just some scrapes."

"He *drowned* at the beach!" Ivan added sadly.

Elena hugged me again. "Oh, no! What would we do without you?" I could think of nothing to say to that and just stayed happily in the hug. She didn't even seem to care that I was getting some open wound effluvia on her robe. "What about your foot?"

"Umm . . . I'm not sure. It *might* have been chomped by a barracuda or something while I was drownding," I lied.

"Pffft!" said Max. "There aren't even barracudas this far north."

"Well, I'm so glad you're okay, my precious John." She lit up a lavender Vogue, exhaling luxuriantly.

To counter my lie, I said, "Elena, Beatriz figured out the entertainment for the Fiesta. We're just going to do stuff we're good at anyway."

Elena said, "I think that's a very sensible plan. I know everybody will love it." She gave us all that big smile we loved, but then squinted at me. "John—your hair! So blond and adorable!"

"I guess the sun bleached it at the beach," I said proudly.

"It's very becoming. We will have to send you to Hollywood to be in the movies, you sexy thing."

Max said, "Yeah. Maybe *Night of the Monster Scab Boy.*"

I sang out, *"What you say is what you are. You're a naked movie star."*

"Sure hope you don't get any flesh-eating screwworms in those little scratches," Max said.

A block over on Raymond Street, we heard Tim's truck, *ding-a-ling-a-ling.* Elena gave us the usual dollar, and we skittered to the street. I forgot to limp. While we waited, I remembered the rubber and showed it off. Max immediately blew it up into a pale balloon, making me and Ivan laugh. Then Tim's truck swung around the corner at the same time Beatriz came running out of her house. She raced Tim up the lane to Ivan's steps, beating him. Max quickly exploded the rubber and pocketed it. Beatriz and Tim saw my pitiful torso at the same time, and Tim said, "Jeez, kid!" Beatriz, out of breath, exclaimed, "John, what *happened*?" I was glad to tell them, but before I could, Leonardo's Olds pulled up, stopping next door at the Allgoods'. "Rumble" twanged darkly from the car radio and was abruptly shut off.

Leonardo and Dawn emerged from the Olds and Leonardo briskly headed for the Allgoods'. Dawn, looking sexy in tight dungarees with a plaid blouse tied at her waist, strolled over to Tim's truck. She stared up at the porch where Elena lay, lazily pushing her swing with one foot and reading a magazine. Dawn called out in an insincere singsong voice, "Leo, I'd *love* a cherry Popsicle," although she looked like she didn't love anything at the moment. Leonardo never broke stride and disappeared into the house.

"Uh-oh," Max whispered to me.

Tim said, a little uncertainly, "Hey, what does everybody want?" He handed Dawn the cherry Popsicle she asked for and she paid, struggling to get the change from her tight jeans, but didn't leave. Tim looked nervous. The humid air thickened with tension and gnats. We waited silently for our treats, swatting and scratching ourselves distractedly. Dawn peeled down her Popsicle wrapper in a slow and deliberate way, and then stood there with a bony hip out, sucking the bloody-red ice lasciviously, glancing at the porch. We couldn't take our eyes off her. Neither could Tim. He wordlessly gave us our usual and finally said, "Take this to your aunt," handing Ivan a Toasted Almond Bar.

We started up the walk when suddenly Dawn shouted, "Hey!" and we all turned to her. "Take *this* to your bitch aunt, too." And she gave Ivan the sideways finger, which was worse than a regular one. Stunned, we watched her stomp away, her ponytail switching angrily from side to side.

His face bright red, Tim said, "Jeez. I don't know *what* that was, but don't let it bother you guys, okay?" He quickly drove off, not jingling at all.

Ivan was as pale as the vanilla ice cream dripping from his uneaten Good Humor.

Beatriz, wide-eyed, whispered, "Yikes! She's *really* scary."

Max rapidly scraped his whole Creamsicle off its stick with his teeth, and, producing the popped rubber, placed the end of it over the top of the stick. Stretching the rubber back, he let it go with a sharp snap, and it sailed over the yews and landed on the Allgoods' walk just as Dawn went into her house, slamming the door. "Take *that,* you scag slut!" Max yelled after her.

"What *was* that thing?" Beatriz asked. "A snakeskin?" We didn't answer. When we turned back to the house, Elena was nowhere to be seen.

10

We reported for duty at the Friedmanns' the next day. I was doing much better; my scabs were dry, the bad foot no longer hurt—much—and I'd almost stopped coughing. Beatriz joined us, and I was glad because I worried about what Max had on his mind, and she was reasonable about things.

The climbing maple was shedding its seeds all around us. Beatriz split a sticky seed and pasted one of its wings on the bridge of her nose, where it protruded like a rhino horn. Ivan did the same.

"It's time to get serious about the vinegaroon," Ivan said very solemnly.

"What are you talking about?" Beatriz said, pasting a rhino horn on Wiesie, who'd come out on the steps. Wiesie tolerated it, perhaps to get back in our good graces after the gigging of Peachy.

I clued Beatriz in about the discovery of the poisonous pirate vinegaroons, and Max told her, "We're going to get one of them and mess Slutcheon up with it."

"Oh, I'd love to do that!" Beatriz said, unfazed. "Remember the time he pulled up my dress and almost goosed me, and I tried to punch him in the face?" I remembered; Beatriz was much braver than we were. "He's a rotten *jagunço*! Where can we find those things?"

"Oh, they're waiting for us at the National Museum," Max said casually, sticking on a rhino horn. "We're going to break in and steal one." He added, "And who said you were coming with us?" He leaned back on his elbows and began humming "Ride of the Valkyries," his favorite tune from a *Merrie Melodies* cartoon featuring Elmer Fudd killing Bugs Bunny. Wagner was verboten in his house.

Beatriz whooped. "Are you *crazy*? *Break into* the museum?" She laughed. "But if you guys go, I go, too."

I groaned. "Max, that's the worst idea you've ever had."

"Well, nobody else has *any* ideas!"

Ivan said, very calmly, "I've thought about it. We were smart enough to get into the Pond Lady's yard, right? It doesn't have to be much differenter or harder than that. We sneak out again at night, ride our bikes down to the museum, get in, and grab it. Just like Nickie in *The Secret Horse*." Ivan and I had a classmate whose mother had written a famous book about a girl who stole a horse. We loved the book, even though it was about a girl.

"But she was stealing a *horse* who was just in a stable, not in a museum," I pointed out. "And she could ride him away. *And* horses aren't poisonous."

—

"Wait a minute! Will those vinegar things *kill* people?" Beatriz wanted to know, fooling nervously with one of her braids.

"Nah," Max answered. "It will only make you sick, and maybe a little bit blind. Unless you're a baby or a geezer, or already sick."

"Okay. I don't want to commit *murder.*" Beatriz crossed herself.

"There are a bunch of people I wouldn't mind being dead," Max said darkly. Ivan nodded.

Beatriz asked, "How do we actually break into the museum?"

Ivan said, "If we go at night, maybe we can pick the lock. We've done that at John's with that thingie his grandfather has." This was another gadget of Brickie's that he called the Hand Jive. "Or we can go at the end of the day before the museum closes, and just hide till everybody's gone and they close up."

"Perfect!" said Max.

Beatriz and I were speechless. Then I asked, "Yeah, Ivan, but how do we *grab* it? I'm sure it's in a glass tank."

"We could wear gloves and smash a hole in the glass with something pointed, like an ice pick. Or a screwdriver. We have to wear gloves anyway so the vinegaroons won't sting us. Remember that guy who stole the Gaboon viper from the zoo? He smashed the glass, too, but he was dumb and put the snake in a pillowcase, and it bit him on the bus when he was trying to get away."

"Won't an alarm go off?" I asked.

"It didn't for the viper guy. He went in during the day and hid till closing time. If an alarm does go off, we're so fast we'll be back on our bikes before a guard or somebody gets there. We can do it! I know we can." I don't think I'd ever seen Ivan so determined, and certainly not about something of this magnitude.

"Hey!" said Max. "My dad has a glass cutter—he's got every tool on earth. It would be easier and quieter than an ice pick."

"Great idea!" Ivan exclaimed.

Beatriz asked Ivan, "Say we get in, and we break the glass case"—that she was now saying "we" instead of "you" was not lost on me—"*then* what do we do? Even if we grab it with gloves it can still spray our eyes, and we might breathe the poison."

"Hmm . . ." Here Ivan was stumped.

"I know!" I was getting enthusiastic. "Swim goggles! I have some!"

So did Ivan and Beatriz, and I said Max could wear Liz's.

"Yeah!" Max said. "And so we don't breathe any, we can tie mouse mattresses across our mouths!" Max had shown me and Ivan bandage-like things his older sister referred to as "mouse mattresses," informing us that girls peed blood every month and had to strap them on.

Beatriz was perplexed, so Max, a little embarrassed, explained what they looked like. "Oh! You mean *Kotex*! Sheesh—boys are so dumb!"

"I'm not putting those things over my mouth," I said. "Why couldn't we just wear bandannas, like the Lone Ranger?"

"Max is right," Ivan said. "Regular cloth might not be thick enough."

"Gah!" I shuddered, wondering why I hadn't seen any mouse mattresses around my house.

"Okay—then what?" Beatriz asked, all business now.

Ivan continued. "Then whoever's wearing gloves has to scootch the boy vinegaroon into a pill bottle and cap it fast."

"What's wrong with catching the girl one?" Beatriz asked.

"The girl one is preggers," I said, using a word I'd heard Liz use. "She's got about thirty eggs on her stomach and we don't need those hatching and running around."

"Although it might be good to have a supply," Ivan mused.

"No, it wouldn't," I said firmly.

Max asked, "After we've trapped the vinegaroon, then what, Ivan?"

"We'll keep him hidden and scare Slutcheon!"

Max spat. "You think Slutcheon won't tell on us? *As if.*"

"Only *scare* him?" said Beatriz.

Max was laughing. "We could put it in a potato-chip sandwich and give it to him!"

I realized that I'd come around to the plan and said, "Or we could sneak it into his clothes, or that little bag on his bike. It won't kill him—it'll just make his life miserable!"

"Yeah!" Max said excitedly. "We'll deny everything! And *he'll* get blamed for stealing it and get sent to Charlotte

Hall!" Charlotte Hall was a frightening military school where out-of-control boys were sent. Brickie occasionally threatened me with it.

Ivan's expression turned doubtful. "The only thing is, how can we get the vinegaroon *back* after it gets Slutcheon?"

I cocked my head quizzically. "Why do we want him back? He'll get squashed as soon as that jerk finds him anyway. Don't be Ivan the Tenderhearted about a vemonous pirate vinegaroon."

"Yeah, but it seems sad. . . . I guess . . . I guess I was thinking it's too bad we can't keep him awhile, after we've made all these plans."

Max shook his head. "*You* made the plan, and it's good. Sometimes you're like Einstein, Ivan. It's almost scary."

"Yeah," I said appreciatively. "You'd make a great Russian spy." Ivan gave me one of his pitiful looks and I quickly amended, "I mean, an *American* spy."

He grinned. "Let's call it the Heist!"

I resignedly pasted a rhino horn on my nose to signal our solidarity.

"When do we do it?" Max asked.

It was odd to have Ivan in charge. But since he was the mastermind of the Heist, we let him figure it out. He said that if we were going to pull it off, it needed to be before school started, with homework, early bedtimes, and more adult scrutiny in general. And with the Fabulous Family Fiesta taking place in a few days, we needed to do it *now*.

"Boys," Beatriz said, "I might know something that will help our plan. I've got ballet now, but I'll tell you more later, okay?" She stroked Wiesie, the furry rhino, and ran off down the lane.

"Bring us something to eat!" Max called. "I shouldn't have even told Beatriz about the vinegaroons," Max said to me. "This is a *boy* job. She doesn't care about spiders."

"She's great at secret stuff! And she's the best liar of all of us, if something happens."

"She is!" Ivan agreed. "Plus, she knows downtown a lot better than any of us."

"Hmpf," said Max. "She better not slow us down."

"She won't," I said stubbornly. Beatriz was fast on her bike and was the first of us to ride with no hands, which had made Max bitter.

"Let's go check out the glass cutter and Brickie's lock picker," I said.

Around the back of the Friedmanns', big wooden barn doors opened to the dirt basement, so we could go right into Mr. Friedmann's workshop, although it was off-limits to us without permission. The workshop walls were hung neatly with garden tools, saws, hammers, spools of wire in all colors, hoses, and contraptions we didn't recognize. Buckets and sacks of fertilizer stood around, organized and labeled in German. Farther back in the dim space, there was a large table. Max opened a wide drawer and held a tool up. "Here's the glass cutter!" It was an eight-inch piece of notched steel, its stem painted orange, with a ball on one end. Max said, "See this little wheel? That's the cutter—you roll it on glass where you want it to cut, it makes a line, and then you tap it with the ball and the glass breaks."

Max sneaked it out under his T-shirt. We then went to my house. I said, "You guys wait here."

I went straight to Brickie's gadget drawer and stole the Hand Jive lock picker. When I was back with the boys, Ivan said, "Let me see." It looked like a fat Swiss Army knife with picks opening out like blades, each one having a different crimped, twisted, or bent end. "I *love* this thing!" Ivan said softly.

There was discussion about which route we'd take for the Heist—we didn't know exactly how to get to the museum; we only knew from trips to the Mall that basically we'd go straight down Connecticut Avenue, but after that it got confusing, as Washington streets often are.

We made a run to the Esso station down at the shopping center and got a free street map and laid it out on Max's porch, crouching over it with a red crayon.

"It looks like the easiest way is down Connecticut, where it turns into Seventeenth Street," Ivan said, tracing the route with the crayon.

I said, "Wow, that's really far, isn't it? That's farther than my dad's apartment when he lived at DuPont Circle."

"We've ridden through Rock Creek Park that far before, don't you think?" Ivan said.

"No, I don't think," Max said. "That *does* look far."

Ivan ignored us both and said, "After that, we're practically right on the Mall. All we do then is get on Constitution Avenue, go down to Tenth Street, and there it is."

Max and I weren't exactly having second thoughts, but it was sinking in that the Heist was now moving swiftly toward reality. Ivan, sensing our misgivings, gave us an odd, steely gaze. "I *know* we can do it."

"Are we going to do it at night, or do like the Gaboon-viper guy and wait till it closes?" I asked him.

"If we do it at closing time, it'll be night anyway," Ivan said. "They're open late in summer."

Beatriz came running hard up the lane, still in her pink leotard, tutu, and tights. Sweaty and excited, she held out a box of Fig Newtons.

Max, surprised, said, "Wow—thanks, Tinkerbell."

She smiled at Max. "You're welcome. Guess what? I checked—my parents will be at a wedding in Georgetown tomorrow, so they'll be drunk and go to bed early, and I can sneak out!"

I was happy to hear it; having Beatriz around gave me courage. Max, his mouth full of Fig Newtons, asked, "So whash thish big idea of yoursh?"

"I've heard my dad talk about this old man named Hampton who goes around to the museums every single night and collects all the tinfoil junk in all the trash cans in the buildings. It's for some crazy thing he's building. He's a janitor at one of the museums, and they all know him, so he's allowed to do it." She stopped to catch her breath for a second. "So if we can go to our museum at night and wait there, the Hampton guy'll probably come, and the door will be open and we can get in easy!"

The boys and I looked at each other. "But what if we miss him?" Ivan asked.

"Well, *then* we might have to pick the lock. But I doubt it, if we just wait."

"But how do we know what door he uses?" I asked her.

"It must be a back one, because wouldn't that be the door a janitor would use?"

"Yeah," Ivan said. "That makes sense. But how do we keep him from seeing us?"

"We just have to be sure he's looking for trash somewhere else in the building when we get in."

We showed Beatriz our tools, and the Esso map. She got down on all fours in her tutu, her butt looking like a big pink flower. With her finger she traced the route Ivan had drawn. "This looks right, I think. But I know how to go without a map—I go to all those museums down there with my dad all the time."

"Okay," said Ivan. "So tomorrow night?" He looked to Max. "We'll spend the night at your house, just like the Pond Lady night?"

"Okay. It'll be Shabbat, so my parents will probably drink a lot of wine and they'll go to bed early, too."

"I'm so excited!" Beatriz jumped up and turned a pirouette. "It'll be like we're in a movie!"

I fervently hoped that our movie wouldn't turn out like *The Asphalt Jungle,* in which most of the thieves died or went to jail.

II

We spent the next morning gathering what we needed for the Heist: Ivan's green pill bottles because they were bigger and the tops were already fixed with air holes, the glass cutter, the Hand Jive, an ice pick just in case, stocking caps from Max—"It's what burglars wear, right?"—goggles, a paper bag to wrap the vinegaroon bottle in, and four Kotex pads Beatriz had stolen from La Senhora and fitted with rubber bands so we could keep them on, and four Hostess CupCakes—"In case we need energy"—from me. Max and I just had thick wool mittens, but Ivan had Elena's red kid gloves, which were lined with fur and fit snugly. All of it was stashed in Max's book bag—he was the only one who had a book bag, because it was required for Hebrew school. I'd have Brickie's penlight in my pocket. We checked and oiled our bikes and covered the reflectors with masking tape. Our darkest clothes were selected, and we figured that long pants would be best so our legs wouldn't stand out. Beatriz would have to wear her Visitation uniform again, because she didn't have any dark pants, but she'd wear her longest kneesocks. Max then complained that her knees would still show, and she said, "At least my skin is *brown*. Your big ghost clown *paleface* is what's gonna show." To counter that, we agreed to smudge her knees and our faces with charcoal from Ivan's grill.

Ivan said, "I think we need to take duct tape so we can cover the hole after we catch him, because we don't want the pregnant one to get out and hurt somebody."

"She's going to die anyway," said Max. "The paper said they die after they have their babies."

"Yeah, but what if she gets out and has the babies and they all attack people at the museum?" Ivan reasoned.

"He's right," I said. "It might bite some little kids. That's called 'collatrial damage,' and that would be bad."

"I'll go get some duct tape." I knew exactly where it would be, from Brickie's threat to tape my mouth on Bachelor Night.

Estelle was in our kitchen, finishing up dinner, which smelled delicious. "Hey, Little Mr. John," she said. Estelle seemed to like cooking more than cleaning. Dimma was always happy to send her home with half of whatever she cooked for us. "What you up to?" she said pleasantly.

"Hi, Estelle." I got the duct tape from the pantry drawer. "We're fixing something." I quickly added, "But we didn't break anything, don't worry. What are you making? It sure smells good."

"Jus' some pot roast, rolls, and things. Your granddaddy loves my pot roast."

"I love it, too!" I said overenthusiastically. "We're spending the night at Max's house, but I'll eat dinner here so I can have some."

"That so?" Estelle said, rolling out some waxed paper to cover the yeast rolls rising on the counter. "Well, y'all have a good time." She added nonchalantly, "And *don't* be creepin' 'round places y'all don't belong."

This worried me, and I hurried out of the kitchen. But realizing Estelle had done us a huge favor by not telling Dimma about the other night's escapade, if she knew, I stuck my head around the corner and said sweetly, "I hope you're coming to our Fiesta."

She stopped what she was doing and turned to me, smiling. "Why, thank you, John. I 'preciate the invitation, but I need my day o' rest. It's a holiday, so I'm gone spend it with my *own* family."

I knew she had a husband, William, who sometimes picked her up, and some older children, but I couldn't have said how many children, or their names. This epiphany made me ashamed—why did I know so little about this woman who knew my family so intimately and did so much for us?

Estelle saw my embarrassment and said kindly, "I *do* plan on makin' deviled eggs and cucumber sandwiches for your comp'ny to enjoy."

"Oh, *good*! Thank you!" We smiled at each other, and I ran back to the boys with the silver tape.

Eleven o'clock was again the appointed hour.

By ten o'clock, all was quiet in Max's house. We three boys were suited up in Max's bedroom, nervously looking at comic books and listening to WDON on Max's transistor. "The Battle of New Orleans" came on, which was pretty much the Shreve boys' anthem. Ivan said, "I *hate* that song." He hated it because Beau and D.L. loved to sing it, but also because the part about grabbing the alligator to use as a cannon—*We filled his head with cannonballs and powdered his behind / And when we touched the powder off the gator lost his mind*—was so cruel. There wasn't much talk, except that Max said, "If we go to reform school, I hope I can have my transistor."

At eleven—zero hour—I looked out the bathroom window and saw Beatriz waiting below with her bike. One by one, we climbed down the maple. Beatriz whispered, "We should go single file, and stay on the sidewalks as much as we can. It's darker, and we'll be hidden better than in the street. I'll go first." She had her braids tucked inside her ski cap and looked like a pretty boy.

Max whispered back nastily, "You should go *last,* Little Brown Dove."

Beatrix stuck out her tongue at him, saying, "*You* don't know the way."

"Well, then, I'll go second because I'm oldest, and *I* have the book bag."

"You're only two weeks older than I am, Max," Beatriz said. I offered to go last, thinking last in line might be first to escape if something went wrong. Beatriz whispered a rapid prayer, "*OmiJesuperdoa-nososnossospercadoenossalvedofogodoinferno,*" kissed the tiny gold saint medal that hung around her neck, and crossed herself.

"Pfft! As if he's going to help you when you're breaking the Eighth Commandment," Max said.

Ivan said, "I don't think God really cares about kids anyway." I was more worried about Brickie than hell, if we got caught. We'd never done anything remotely as foolhardy.

Max produced the hunk of charcoal and we passed it around, helping one another rub it on our faces and Beatriz's skinny knees.

We started off hesitantly at first, taking our school route down Raymond, then turning left onto Connecticut and speeding up. We passed the Chevy Chase Club on the right, and then Lenox Street and Kirke Street, the fancier neighborhood, where Slutcheon and Gellert lived. We passed Blessed Sacrament at Chevy Chase Circle, where the splash of the fountain played forcefully; the splash of it was loud and clear in the almost-empty night. I remembered the time some hoods put detergent in the water and foam covered everything. The Avalon Theatre still had lights on, doing away with the shadows, but the people in the handful of cars that passed seemed not to notice us. Racing along, we passed large, older houses alternating with newer apartment buildings—Sulgrave Manor, a very modern building, then Clarence House, where Dr. Spire had his Chamber of Shots, then Connecticut Hot Shoppes. Then the Yenching Palace, with its cool diamond windows, where a waiter cleaning up waved at us, and the Uptown Theater, where I'd seen *The Monolith Monsters* with my dad.

Everybody's legs were churning hard, and we flew along, our pedaling synchronized and our bodies hunched over our handlebars. The night air was cool and invigorating; I wasn't even sweating. I'd still been a little sore from my drowning, but I felt invincible now. We whizzed past groups of row houses, the old Kennedy-Warren apartments, and then we passed the zoo and the Shoreham Hotel, high on the hill, the grounds brightly lit. Beatriz stuck her arm out, signaling left, and we moved to the other side of the street. Coming to the Taft Bridge, its fancy streetlights illuminated it like daytime. Too many cars were coming across. Beatriz signaled for us to stop. We pulled into the dark weeds and shrubs just before the bridge.

Beatriz said, "Let's rest a second."

"I knew she'd slow us down," Max said, although he was breathing as hard as the rest of us.

Beatriz snapped back, "The bridge is too bright! We need to wait till these cars are gone." Waiting, trying to catch our breath, we admired the eagles on the tops of the streetlights, and the giant lions guarding the bridge. I thought I could see the minaret of the mosque on Massachusetts Avenue in the distance, its crescent a little moon in the sky.

With a lull in the traffic, we shoved off again, going through Kalorama, with its swankier houses and apartments, and then passing S Street, where Holton-Arms was, and then the Golden Parrot, where Liz and I'd had dinner with my father and I'd acted like a brat because they didn't serve hamburgers, and R Street, where Daddy used to live.

Suddenly, a taxi waiting in front of the restaurant pulled away from the sidewalk and began driving alongside us. A man with a grouchy face rolled down the driver's window and yelled, "Hey, you kids! What're you doing out here so late? Pull over!" *Oh, no,* I thought—*we're done for.* Beatriz rose from her bike seat, standing on her pedals to speed away. We followed her lead, but the taxi driver cut in front of Beatriz, who stopped short with a scrunch of her tires, bumping into the side of the cab. We boys crashed into each other, one after the other, like dominoes. The taxi driver looked us up and down. "What are you boys up to? It can't be anything good at this time of night."

Beatriz coolly replied, "No, sir. We were in a school play tonight. These are our costumes. We're on our way home."

"Oh, yeah? Where is home?"

"Right down there," I piped up, pointing to the Circle. "We're spending the night at my dad's house."

After a moment, the man said, oddly friendly now, "Do you want a ride? I can pile your bikes in the trunk." He smiled, but it was not a good smile.

Max spoke up. "That's okay. We're almost there."

"Well, get on down there before the cops pick you up." He rolled up his window and pulled away. We watched to be sure he was gone.

"Whew," I said. "That was close."

"Yeah," Max said grimly. "*Too* close. That guy was *creepy.*"

At DuPont Circle there was a lot of seedy nightlife—people hanging out, making deals, laughing and drinking. Nobody paid us any attention. We rounded the Circle, then passed the Tiny Jewel Box—a lovely old brick house with a dome, where Brickie often bought Dimma birthday or Christmas presents, and then the Mayflower Hotel. At L Street we went by Duke Zeibert's, one of my dad's hangouts, and then Farragut Square, where Connecticut curved into Seventeenth Street. Passing Admiral Farragut's statue, Max stupidly hollered out, "Damn the torpedoes! Full speed ahead!" At this point I really hoped that Beatriz knew what she was doing, because I no longer did, and I knew Ivan and Max didn't, either. Passing the Renwick Gallery, Beatriz gave a thumbs-up. I felt even better when we passed a massive fortress, pompously ornate with its columns: an obvious government building and a sign that we were getting close. We zipped by the Corcoran, and the O.A.S. building, where I remembered that Elena often went to parties. There, the Mall opened before us, the Washington Monument rising up, gleaming like a giant sword. Beatriz signaled a left turn, and we cruised down Constitution, past more offices, arriving at Tenth Street, where, on our right, the National Museum loomed over us.

We pulled off into some trees, grinning at one another, chests heaving. We were silent for a moment, catching our breath. The Mall was very eerie and deserted; I'd never seen it when it wasn't bustling with sightseers.

"It's too *quiet,*" I said, a little spooked. "There aren't even any crickets. Or lightning bugs. And no webs."

Max said, "They're all dead! I bet they dropped some of that Smear 62 junk to get rid of the spiders and vinegaroons."

"It's *good* that it's quiet," said Beatriz. "That's what we want!"

Ivan, a hand clutching his crotch, whispered urgently, "I've got to pee!" He laid down his bike and peed with his back to us. Zipping up, he said, "Now we look for a back door. Walk our bikes."

I asked Ivan, "The Zoology Hall is on the right, isn't it?"

"It was when we came to see the new elephant with Elena," he said.

We started around the right side of the museum. "Looks like there's a light on back there," I said. "Is that good or bad?" At the corner of the building was a large boxwood, and under its cover we peeked around to see light pouring out from a door propped open with a big trash can. A dark-green Ford pickup truck with a government logo on its door and an old maroon Plymouth were parked in the service drive. More trash cans stood by the truck. Max said, "There must be people inside!"

I whispered, *"Duh!"*

"But maybe they're leaving," Ivan said. Ivan and Max waited, then craned their necks around the corner to look again. Nobody.

"It's gotta be the Hampton guy!" said Beatriz.

"Maybe," Ivan said. "But there must be somebody else, too."

"Should we wait and see, or try to go in now?" I whispered.

"Let's wait a few minutes," Ivan said.

"I say we try to get in *now,*" Max said. "Then we won't have to try to pick the lock."

"Max, if we go in now, we might run right into whoever's in there. Let's just see what's happening," Ivan responded.

Beatriz said, "I'm with Ivan—just wait a minute."

Ivan directed us, "Leave our bikes here, behind the bush.

Don't use the kickstands, just turn them around and lean them against the wall so we can hop on fast when we go." We did this as quietly as we could. We waited.

Nothing happened, and then nothing happened some more. All of a sudden there were crashing and scraping noises from the open door. My heart banged in my chest. Beatriz clutched my arm. A man in a suit came out, followed by a tall, dark-skinned man in a uniform dragging two trash cans. "Good night, Hampton," the suit man said. "Hope you find some things you can use." Setting the trash cans by the others, the uniformed man said, "'Night, Dr. Smith. I'm 'bout to finish up. See you tomorrow."

"That's him! That's Hampton!" Beatriz squeezed my arm hard.

The suit guy got in his Plymouth, cranked it, and turned on the headlights.

"Get down!" Ivan hissed. We hit the pavement, hoping that the boxwood hid us. The car turned around in the service drive, its headlights swooping across the boxwood, and drove off.

Hampton reached into the open window of his truck and switched on the radio. Gospel music played loudly—a woman singing throatily about being on her way. "He's gonna leave soon! Get ready!" Ivan whispered. We stood back up. But Hampton went back inside and after a few minutes returned with two more trash cans. He stopped and reached into his truck again, bringing out a paper sack and a pack of cigarettes. He lit one, sucked on it, and opened the bed of his truck. Then Hampton began sorting through the trash, bringing up glinting pieces of aluminum foil—sandwich wrappers, insides of cigarette packs, Wrigley's gum papers—and sticking them in his sack. He stopped to draw on his smoke a couple more times, then tossed it. He began singing along to the song. Picking up one of the big cans, he shoved it in the truck bed, then leapt up after it, taking time to carefully situate it. Then he jumped down and picked up another can and did the same. There were several more trash cans.

Ivan whispered fiercely, "When he jumps up in the truck the next time, we go!" Hampton toted another can, and when he clambered up into the truck bed again, still singing along loudly to the radio, Ivan said, *"Now!"*

On tiptoes, we ran around the corner as fast and quietly as we could and were inside the open door in a split second. Another full can sat inside, and Ivan, leading, almost ran into it. We kept going: down a hall past an open cleaning closet, past a lot of other doors, and a bathroom, coming to a flight of stairs. "We must be in the basement—go up!" Ivan said. We scrambled up, ending up in the dark of the main rotunda, where arcades branched off, interspersed with swirly marble columns. There stood the wondrous new African elephant Elena had taken us to see. It was scary to us now, in the dark. Ivan pointed into the closest arcade and we skittered in and stopped, pressing our backs to the wall. I could hear our labored breathing. We waited silently, still able to hear the radio playing outside. Ivan said, "Keep still!" After a few minutes, we heard the loud slam of a door, and the radio stopped.

Max whispered, "You think he's leaving?" Nobody answered him, and we stood there a few more minutes.

"Wait till we hear his truck crank up," I said.

We waited. There were no sounds at all. Finally, we heard the engine start.

"I think he's gone," Ivan said. He turned to Max and Beatriz. "You two wait here and keep watch. If you hear someone coming, give a little whistle, and everybody hide." This was a good idea; Max was too much of a loose cannon, and Beatriz could be trusted to keep him in line, and nobody needed to be alone.

"Hey!" Max protested. "I've got the bag!"

"We'll signal you when we find it," Commander Ivan said. He yanked me back into the rotunda with him. "Get out your light."

I pulled out my little penlight and clicked it on as we began creeping around. We were pretty sure the insect exhibits were on the right, in a room off the rotunda, but we couldn't recall which one. I flashed my penlight across the tops of the arches, looking for a sign, but the light wasn't strong enough for us to read them. We moved closer, FOSSILS, ANTHROPOLOGY. Then ZOOLOGY.

"Yay!" I said.

Ivan and I entered the room. Then, from back where we'd left Beatriz and Max, a door slammed, followed by a short, low-pitched whistle. Ivan and I panicked and scuttled to the wall just inside the room, pressing back against it. I turned off my light, my heart galloping crazily. After nothing happened, Ivan hesitantly looked out toward where we'd left Max and Beatriz. His loud whisper expanded around the rotunda, "Max, what's wrong?"

"*Beatriz* had to go to the bathroom back there, and she let the door slam! I thought it was someone coming in!"

"Sorry!" she whispered back.

Ivan answered, "We think it's here! Come to the light!" I switched on the pen, pointing it at the floor. They tiptoed over.

"Shouldn't *one* of us still stand guard?" I questioned. Simultaneously Max and Beatriz said, "Not me!" Nobody wanted to miss the Heist, or stand alone in the dark.

Ivan said, "If somebody comes, we separate, get out of here, jump on our bikes, and leave—don't wait for anybody! There's no point in *all* of us getting caught."

The idea unnerved me, but I got the logic of it and said, "And if someone *does* get caught, nobody rats on anybody else, right?" We all agreed.

The four of us advanced together into the insect room, looking around as if there might be a neon sign illuminating the celebrity pirate vinegaroons. We went from case to case, following my penlight, looking for the prize. Halfway around the room, I cried, "Here it is! It's this one!" We all crowded together. A placard on the exhibit case read PIRATE VINEGAROON; under this was its Latin name, UROPYGI PIRATA. The legend beneath told a shorter version of all the information we'd read in the papers. The words EXTREMELY POISONOUS stood out.

Peering into the case, Beatriz said, "There's nothing in there but rocks!"

"They're hiding," Ivan said. "They're reclusive."

"Shine the light back here." Max was looking all over, beneath and behind the exhibit case. "I don't see any wires or plugs anywhere, so there must not be an alarm."

"Let's get our stuff on," I said. Max took the book bag from around his neck, setting it on the floor. He handed Ivan Elena's red gloves and gave each of us a mouse mattress tied with a rubber band. "Gah! I can't believe we're wearing these!" I said.

"Just let them hang around our necks till we need them," Beatriz ordered.

Out came the goggles, too, and we put them on. With our burglar caps, we looked like we were operatives on a top-secret, dangerous mission. Which I guess we were.

"We actually need to be more worried about getting bitten than sprayed. The *bite's* what makes you *really* sick," Ivan pointed out.

"How are we going to get them to come out of the rocks?" Beatriz asked.

"Maybe if I shine my light, it'll attract them, like bug zappers do?"

"Try it," Max said. I did, and we waited. "Come *out,* you morons."

"Do you think they could've killed each other?" I wondered.

Nothing stirred. "Rats!" Ivan said angrily. "Why didn't we bring some beetles to attract them?"

"I know!" Max said. "The Hostess CupCakes!" He rummaged in the bag and drew the package out, unwrapped it, and broke off a cakey crumb. "When we break the case, I'll toss this in. They'll come out to investigate."

Beatriz asked Ivan, "Where will you make the hole?"

"At the bottom-left corner, like this." He traced his finger horizontally from the left side of the case to the right about three inches, and then down to the bottom the same length, and up the case frame. "I'll have to cut a whole square." He looked at his hand. "The hole needs to be small and tight so the girl can't run up my arm while I catch the boy, and you guys have to tape it fast. Max, you should tear off a bunch of duct-tape strips and be ready with them." Beatriz helped Max with the tape, the ripping sound echoing spookily around the room. He stuck the strips lightly to his arm.

We stood silently for a moment. Ivan drew a deep breath and said, "Okay. I'm going in. Gimme the glass cutter. You guys be ready with a pill bottle, cap, and tape." He drew on Elena's red gloves and Max handed him the cutter. I felt goose bumps all over. Beatriz crossed herself.

I shined the light on the spot. Ivan very slowly began rolling the blade of the cutter across the glass. It wasn't making the white etched line Max said it was supposed to. "Put more pressure on it," Max said. Ivan tried again, leaning in. No line. *"Oh, no,"* Max whispered. "I forgot! The wheel has to be lubricated. My dad puts oil on it." Ivan drew back and spat a wad of saliva onto the wheel. He ran the cutter along the four sides of the square, and the lines appeared. He stepped back for a second, taking a deep breath. "You guys ready?" Turning the tool around, he tapped on the glass along the lines with the ball end, gently at first, then harder. The glass wouldn't give. Frustrated, Ivan punched more forcefully, and the glass finally broke, but not cleanly. The square cutout fell back into the case, a few jagged pieces standing up from the frame like shark teeth. Ivan gingerly snapped them off.

"Einstein!" Max whispered.

"Throw in the cake, Max! Close to the hole, but not too close." Max stepped forward and tossed in the crumb, quickly backing away.

More waiting. Ivan took off his jacket, saying, "If they come running out too fast, I'll stuff the hole with this." Then we saw movement in the rocks. I pointed the light so it wasn't directly on the rocks. Purple claws slowly emerged, first one set from the left, then one from the right.

"Put on the mouse mattresses!" Beatriz cried. We pulled the Kotex pads up over our noses and mouths.

"There they are!" I exclaimed. The vinegaroons crept out, raising their claws high as they came forward. They were even more frightening than they were in the photos. Beatriz shuddered against me.

Ivan said excitedly, his voice muffled by the Kotex, "That's the girl on the right! Look—her eggs hatched! There're *tons* of them!" A crowd of wriggling babies piggybacked on the mother.

"Man!" said Max. "They look like tiny white squids!"

"Oh, the poor thing!" said Beatriz.

"We only want the boy," I said firmly, hoping Ivan wasn't still thinking of having a *supply*. "And he's closest to the hole."

"He needs to come closer," Ivan said, tugging at his left glove.

The creatures advanced toward the cake, the male leading. Beatriz said, "Of *course* the boy's going to hog the food."

The male reached the cake, about three inches back. He snatched it in his pincers, then chomped it with his black, venom-packed fangs. The female continued forward.

"Ivan!" I cried. "Catch him before she gets close! Quick!"

Ivan seemed paralyzed. "Hurry, Ivan!" Max urged him. "Do you want me to do it?" He gave Ivan's arm a nudge. The female kept advancing.

"I'm okay—I'm doing it. Stand right here to hand me the pill bottle, and be ready with the cap." He slowly began putting his gloved left hand through the hole. The male vinegaroon dropped the crumb and waved his claws menacingly, poising his tail.

I could feel Beatriz shaking, or maybe it was me.

Just as Ivan's hand neared the male, the female rushed forward, claws raised. "Ivan!" I cried. He seized the male and tried to withdraw his hand, but the hole was too small for his clenched fist. He dropped the vinegaroon, and the creature scuttled backward toward his mate. *"Mierda!"* Ivan cried. All his bravado evaporated. He was on the verge of tears.

"Look! I thought we might need this!" From her sweater, Beatriz drew a small green net, its wire handle bent to fit in her sweater pocket. Her voice trembling, she said, "I use it for my fish when I clean their tank. Do you want to try it?"

But Ivan was through. "No—you do it. Maybe your hands are smaller." He took off the red gloves and Beatriz put them on, then bent the wire so that the net was at a right angle to its handle. Max and I exchanged a glance, and I know he was as relieved as I was that he and I were spared.

"Ready with the bottle and cap?" Beatriz asked me. I nodded, wanting badly to clutch my pants.

Beatriz extended her hand, holding the little net, until it passed through the square hole. She steadily moved toward the vinegaroons. They both raised their whiptails and sprayed. Beatriz gently flicked the female away, then rapidly dropped the net over the male. Slowly, slowly, she dragged him along the gravelly bottom, then over to the edge of the hole. "Give me the bottle. Have the tape and paper bag ready." She took the green bottle from me with her free hand and held it next to the trapped vinegaroon. With one swift move, she scooched him into the bottle, then snatched the cap from me and screwed it on. I held the paper bag open, and she dropped the pill bottle inside, then rolled the bag into a tight cigar. Max jumped over with the duct-tape strips he'd readied on his sleeve and quickly patched the hole. There was the sharp smell of vinegar.

"Get away from the case!" I said, backing off.

"Take this thing, Ivan!" Beatriz thrust the rolled-up bag at him and tore off Elena's gloves.

We scurried to gather up our stuff, jamming everything into Max's book bag. The Kotex pads were slipping down off our faces, and I all but shouted, "Hold your breath! Pull the caps over your faces!"

With the caps pulled over our goggles, we were blind, stumbling and bumping into each other. Someone fell heavily against me and crashed to the floor, crying *"Mierda!"* again. I yanked Ivan up and we slammed into a wall.

Max yanked up his cap for a second, looking around, and said, "Everybody hold hands. We're going back the way we came. Stay against the wall."

We followed Sergeant Max's directions like kindergarteners. I was between Beatriz and Ivan, our hands slick with sweat. Still blind, we spilled down the steps, groping along the basement hall. At the back door, we ripped off our goggles and caps, Beatriz's braids tumbling out. "My head is *boiled*!"

Ivan whimpered, "I think I might've *smushed* him when I fell!"

We looked at each other in horror. I said, "We have to check him."

Ivan withdrew the paper sack jammed in his pocket, opening it cautiously. The vinegar smell was overpowering. "Pew!" I said, an elbow over my face. Ivan held up the intact pill bottle, and I shined my light on it. In the limited space the vinegaroon had, he moved his claws.

"Graças a Deus!" Beatriz whispered.

"Let's get the aitch outta here," Max said urgently. "Put him on *top* of the junk in my book bag, so if something happens on the way home, I can just ditch it if I have to." We threw in our headgear, placing the vinegaroon on top. Max said, "Just leave the mouse mattresses so they'll think some *girls* stole the vinegaroon."

Beatriz said huffily, "*Some girl* did steal it!"

"Let's go." I looked at the push bar of the door for a second and went cold. "You guys—what if we're locked *in,* or the door sets off an alarm?"

Max cried impatiently, *"Just do it!"* I cranked the bar down slowly, pushing. It didn't open. I looked back at everybody, all their mouths agape, eyes wide. My heart thundered in my ears. Max stepped up and leaned against the door, pushing the bar harder. It didn't give. His face was dripping, and he stopped to wipe it on his sleeve.

"We didn't think about fingerprints," Ivan whispered.

"The FBI doesn't keep kids' fingerprints," Max said. "*Do* they?" Then, heaving his whole weight against the door, he cranked the bar powerfully, grunting with the effort. The door opened. We froze, waiting for an alarm, but heard only our breathing.

"I knew the angels would look out for us!" Beatriz whispered.

"Let's go!" said Max. We burst out the door and scrabbled around the corner to our bikes by the boxwood, hearing the door slam behind us. Max said, "We'll ride back the way we came, but remember, if someone's after us, split up!" We hopped on our bikes, quickly pedaling to the street.

With new energy fueled by fear and adrenaline, we zipped a couple blocks along Constitution Avenue, avoiding the streetlights. Suddenly there were headlights behind us. I looked back. "It's Hampton's truck!" I called out. Max was leading, and we veered off onto the Mall, where we stopped in the shadows behind a tree. The truck slowed down, but we couldn't make out whether or not Hampton was looking our way.

Max said, "If he gets out and comes for us, I'm dumping the vinegaroon!" The truck came flush with us and stopped. "Damn!" I whispered, afraid I might wet my pants. "We're doomed!"

A match flared in the blackness inside the cab. "He's just lighting a cigarette, *Advice Lady,*" Max hissed at me. The truck rolled on by. We waited until it picked up speed and turned out of sight. Then we were off again.

The return trip seemed much faster. There were practically no cars at all, not even at DuPont Circle or the Taft Bridge. I desperately longed for my bed, or at least Max's. I was still terrified, but felt less so with every block. Whizzing up Connecticut Avenue, closing in on Chevy Chase, we were traveling so fast I felt like I was having one of those flying dreams. I was just beginning to relish our triumph when there was a shriek, a *whump,* and a crash as Beatriz, riding ahead of me, flew into the air and came down with her bike on top of her, its wheels spinning. "Help!" she cried as I slammed to a stop where she lay on the edge of someone's lawn.

"Beatriz!" I shouted, too loud.

Max and Ivan, far ahead, skidded to a stop. "What happened?" Max called. I was trying to pull the bike off her and help her up.

"Ow! Ow! Don't pull on me! I'm stuck!" she said, crying a little. "The sidewalk—I hit that big hump." Just behind her, a huge tree root heaved up the sidewalk. Max and Ivan had jumped it, or swerved around it in time. They came running back to help. We saw that one of her long braids was tangled in her front bike wheel, wound tightly around the center of the spokes. Max tried to work it free but got nowhere. Beatriz cried, "Guys—I'll untangle it somehow! *Go on*!"

"Gah! What do we do?" I panicked and couldn't think.

"We can't just leave her!" Max said.

Then Ivan, looking grim, pulled his pocketknife out. Opening the blade, he bent close to her. He said, very deliberately, "Beatriz. I have to. Or we'll all get caught. I'm *so sorry*."

Beatriz looked horrified.

I didn't understand and cried, "Ivan! What . . . what are you doing?" I had an insane vision of Ivan slashing her throat so we could get away.

Max squawked, "What's *wrong* with you, Ivan?"

When Ivan grasped the tangled braid and said, "It's got to go," Max and I heaved huge sighs of relief.

But Beatriz wasn't relieved, pleading, "Not my *hair*! My parents will *murder* me!"

Ivan repeated, "I'm sorry! We'll think of something to tell your mom!" Lights came on in the house at the back of the lawn.

Ivan sawed and hacked at the braid just below her ear. Then he yanked hard, and her head bounced as it was freed from the spokes. He handed Beatriz the dead braid as Max jerked her bike up. "Your bike's fine! Quick! We gotta go!"

I asked her, "Can you ride okay?"

"I think so." But she didn't sound sure. "My knee hurts."

I got behind Beatriz to be sure nothing else happened to

her. As we pedaled off, a man's angry voice came from the house: "Who's out there?"

Max led us across Connecticut, and we vanished into the shadows of a side street. We circled back to the Avalon—the home stretch—and in a few minutes we were back on Connors Lane, cruising to Max's.

Safely under the climbing maple, we were shell-shocked and shaking. The enormity of what we'd accomplished hadn't set in.

Beatriz thought she was only a little sore. "My kneesocks kept my legs from getting too scraped." But she did have a raw place speckled with sidewalk crud on her knee.

"Why didn't your *angels* see that bump?" Max taunted.

We all looked at Beatriz, with her one braid hanging sadly. Ivan asked her, "Don't you think I should cut off your other braid?"

She thought for a second and said miserably, "You might as well. I'll put my cap back on to sneak back into my house, but what am I gonna tell them in the morning?" She was ready to cry.

"Why don't you tell them that you saw a picture of a really cute Girl Scout in *Seventeen* with a short haircut, and that they called her the 'New American Girl,' and you just wanted to look more American?" I suggested, having seen that exact feature in Liz's latest copy of *Seventeen.*

Beatriz said, "I don't think my parents *want* me to look more American."

Max offered, "Tell them it's too hot and way too much

trouble to have long hair, and that you'd rather spend more time on your cataclysm."

"It's *catechism.* A cataclysm is like when the Russians blow us up," Beatriz corrected, issuing a snuffly laugh. "I know—I'll tell them I'll go to confession, too. I hope they don't punish me by not letting me go to the Fiesta."

Ivan whipped out his trusty knife and, with trembling hands, chopped off the other braid, giving it to Beatriz. "Wow," she whispered. "My head feels so *light*!"

"I hope you get inside okay," I said. "Don't forget to wash the charcoal off."

"Okay," she said, smiling. "What an adventure!" She rode back down the lane.

"Uhh . . . my head feels light, too." Ivan sat down, then lay back in the dirt. "My chest hurts."

"Ivan!" I was afraid for him. "We have to get you into bed!" Max and I fanned him frantically with our hands. His white face practically glowed in the dark.

After a few minutes, he said, "I think I'm okay now." We helped him up the tree, but he was pretty weak.

We tiptoed fast to the bathroom, where we all took elephantine pees, then we stripped down and quietly got in a cold shower, rinsing the charcoal off. In Max's bedroom the clock said 1:07. Max turned on the fan to obscure any noise. I'd never been so exhausted in my life—well, maybe after I drowned. Ivan seemed rejuvenated—a little—by the shower, but sat on the floor. Max whispered joyfully, "*You guys—we did it!* Are we not the three coolest cats in the *world*?"

"Re-*mark*-able! We heisted the vinegaroon!" We were

suddenly jubilant, and Max and I performed a silent victory dance, like naked cavemen after a kill. Ivan only watched, grinning. Then we all put on our underpants and threw ourselves onto Max's bed.

"I want to see him one more time," said Ivan.

Max rose back up and grabbed the paper bag from his book bag. "Gah! It still reeks!" He proffered it to Ivan. Ivan unwrapped the paper-sack cocoon and took out the green pill bottle, holding it to the streetlight. The vinegaroon moved a bit, and Ivan said, "Ta-da!"

Max spoke to the vinegaroon. "Aargh, matey! You'll soon be making Slutcheon walk the plank!" He clacked his tongue, *"Tick tock, tick tock!"* like the evil crocodile that plagued Captain Hook.

"Max, do you have a Magic Marker?" Ivan asked.

"I think so. Somewhere." He pawed through a drawer and found one.

Ivan sat on the edge of the bed, hunched over the bottle. Very meticulously he drew a small skull and crossbones on the plastic.

"Like you might *forget* there's something poisonous in there?" I said.

"It's just in case," said Ivan. "And he's a *pirate* vinegaroon. Pirates always have a skull and crossbones on their stuff, right?"

Max said, "Okay, now get that thing outta my bed."

"Just one good-night kiss." Ivan smooched at the bottle and replaced it on the sill sideways, shoring it up with the

Magic Marker. For a moment we admired our trophy, silhouetted against the streetlight, the bottle glowing like an emerald.

I cautioned, "You better be *super* careful with him because of the twins and the dogs."

Wiesie traipsed in, sniffed around, hunching her back and hissing like a Halloween cat, and ran out of the room. Max yawned, saying, "John and I thought for a second you were going to *kill* Beatriz, Ivan."

"Oh, brother! Maybe your brains *did* get poisoned," he said and laughed. I considered this and started to worry not only about the vinegaroon's welfare, but about everybody else's. And I worried about Ivan's sinking spell. But I was overtaken by a yawn. I should have been *very* worried, as things turned out.

The clock said 1:26. We conked out, too battle-fatigued to laugh, scratch, or even dream.

12

Two mornings later it was the day of the Fabulous Family Fiesta, and the temperature was already ungodly high. It had stormed during the night, and with my obsessive dread of lightning, I'd woken up in a panic. I hadn't run to my grandparents' room to sleep on the floor between their beds like I usually did because I could see, between flashes, the palest beginnings of morning just beyond the locust trees in our backyard. I had a skinny little book that featured illustrations of a phenomenon called black lightning, and a fireball coming through a window and rolling across the floor, just like the A-bomb fireballs we'd learned about in civil-defense drills. I'd planned to saturate the book with lighter fluid and incinerate it in the stone fireplace at the bottom of our yard. I was so afraid of the book that I hadn't burned it yet.

Ivan and I were despondent about the weather. We'd worked too hard—or *we* thought we had—planning, putting up posters, and worrying about entertainment, to cancel. But yards were muddy, branches dripped, and the spiderwebs that still hung over the neighborhood were strung with raindrops. A thick, sunless haze made it seem hard to breathe. Steam rose off our mossy walk and clouds of gnats were already bothering us. Max tried to be optimistic, saying, "Don't worry. It'll dry up by Fiesta time."

Ivan said, "How do you know it won't rain more?" He pointed at some heavy clouds in the distance, no doubt packed with black lightning. He was bleary-eyed and pale, but seemed to have recovered from the Heist.

"Because I know—I heard the Joy Boys say it on the radio last night."

"Yeah, but I asked my Magic 8-Ball if it was going to be a nice day, and it said, *'My sources say no,'*" I complained. I was also disappointed, and so was Max, because Slutcheon hadn't come by for his just deserts the day after the Heist, but Ivan just seemed glad to have the vinegaroon.

We'd spent the day before sleeping late, resting on our hard-earned laurels, and waiting not only for Slutcheon but for Gary, the paperboy, to come around in his noisy red-and-white Nash Rambler and deliver the *Star.* When it arrived, we unfolded it nervously, scanning the front page for news of the Heist. There, at the bottom, we saw: RARE SCORPION STOLEN FROM MUSEUM. Clustered together, we read that authorities were very concerned and had no real leads, museum employees who'd been working late that night said they hadn't noticed anything amiss, and local hospitals had no reports of anyone being treated for vinegaroon exposure. Naturally, there was speculation that Russians might have been involved. Max had said, "Why would the Russians steal it *back*?" Reading on, we took exception to the part about "chocolate cake used as an amateurish baiting method" by the thief, and that the exhibit case had been "inexpertly cut and patched." But we loved the detail that there was also speculation that a woman may have committed the crime, but it didn't say why.

"If Slutcheon comes to the Fiesta today," I asked, "could we do it then?"

"No!" Ivan cried. "I mean, then everybody would know it was somebody at the Fiesta who broke into the museum. And *we're* the most likely suspects."

"That's true," Max agreed.

Ivan was adamant. "We just need to wait till the right time!"

At that moment Brickie stepped out onto our steps and said, "Jesus Christ, the mug out here is thicker than *drisheen*," which was some Irish crap his mother had forced him to eat as a child. "I guess I can expect a major efflorescence of fungus on the last of my bee balm and zinnias." The morning *Post* was tucked under his arm. "The paper says it'll be clear tonight. Shouldn't you boys be busy getting ready?"

I ignored the question and asked, "Why do you have to work today? It's Labor Day."

"That's right—it's *Labor* Day. I have to go *labor.* That's your government—always at work so Americans have the freedom to lounge around on holidays. Right, guys?"

"Right," we answered.

"By the way, did you boys hear about that whip-scorpion

creature that was stolen from the National Museum the other night?"

"Yeah," I said casually. "That's pretty cool. Did they find any fingerprints?"

"Today's *Post* says they found some, but they were small—maybe teenagers. If I didn't know you boys better, I'd think *you* stole it!" Brickie laughed. "See you this afternoon. Please don't give your grandmother too much trouble." He went off in his black government Dodge Coronet.

We looked at each other, bug-eyed. "See?" said Ivan. Max gave a low whistle of relief.

"I guess we should start doing stuff," I said.

Max said, "All we really have to do is fix up the cake, mix up the Kool-Aid, and put up some decorations—I don't know what."

"We need tables for food and stuff," I said. "And chairs. It might be too wet for people to sit on blankets."

We took a few minutes for some scratching. A mourning cloak flitted by—they were flying so slowly at this time of year—and rested on a nearby azalea bush. I caught it gently in my hands. I didn't have a mourning cloak in my butterfly collection, and its amazing gold and blue colors and deckled wings put me in mind of a skirt of my mother's, and this made me a little sad. For Ivan's sake, I let it go. Beautiful butterfly dust was all over my hands, so I stroked it onto my cheeks. What I really wanted to do was put it on my eyelids, like Elena. "War paint!" said Ivan.

"Let's go see the vinegaroon," Max said.

"This morning he ate a *cucaracha*," Ivan said proudly.

We hustled across the street to the Goncharoffs', sneaking stealthily up to Ivan's room, where he carefully took the shoe box containing the vinegaroon down from his closet shelf. He'd fixed the top with a viewing hole covered with plastic wrap, and furnished the box with sand and rocks. The vinegaroon rested peacefully in his green bottle hidey-hole. Max quickly threw in one of Tallulah's beetles, and he scuttled out, grabbed it, and started gobbling it with his black fangs. "So cool!" I said.

Max added, "You're gonna love the taste of Slutcheon, old buddy!"

"Ivan, you gotta be *sure* to keep him hidden." The other night's inkling of fear still crept around in my head like a poison-ivy vine. Then I asked a question I wasn't sure I wanted to hear the answer to. "How's Elena?"

"She's okay . . . I guess." Changing the subject, he said, "Let's go downstairs to see if Maria has the cake ready."

In the stifling kitchen, a sweaty Maria was just taking a big yellow rectangle of cake out of the oven. *"Caliente!"* she warned. "*Cuando está frío,* you make pretty." Rudo and Linda and the toddler twins ran in, Katya and Alexander babbling in Spanish. Maria gave the four of them fresh tortillas and they scrabbled back to the yard, dog toenails clicking on the floor, tortillas flapping.

Ivan spoke to Maria in Spanish and she answered, wiping her face with her apron. Ivan translated, "We gotta wait two hours till the cake cools, then we can ice it. Let's go collect chairs and things." He grabbed up two small Mexican chairs painted brightly with flowers, and we dumped them in my yard.

"We need to check on Beatriz," I said. We hadn't seen her since the Heist. We were hesitant to knock on the door, fearing the Senhor and Senhora, so Max just called out, "Be-a-trizzz!" She appeared at the back door, and it was something of a shock. There was an angry scab on her knee, and her hair was now trimmed in a short Darla-esque bob. "Everything is okay," she whispered. "I told my parents what you and Max said, and they believed it. I had to go get my hair fixed yesterday. At first they were mad, but I think they like my new look, and Zariya got hers cut, too!" She struck a movie star pose, poofing up her bob.

"It looks great!" I said, and Max agreed, saying, a little wistfully, "You sure don't look like Little White Dove anymore." We'd all miss those shiny black braids.

"Are you guys okay? What about the you-know-what?"

"Everybody's fine." Ivan smiled.

"What you boys *need* to be doing is getting ready for the Fiesta!" So bossy, but thank God for Beatriz.

"That's what we're doing!" I said.

Ivan said sheepishly, "You saved the day the other night, Beatriz. Thanks."

"Yeah, you were pretty brave," Max said.

"We were *all* brave! We all did our part! Hey—let me get the decorations I made." She ran off, returning with a stack of colorful paper flags. "They're the flags of all the neighbors' countries! America, Brazil, Holland, Austria, Ukraine, England, Mexico, and Hungaria, for Gellert!"

she said excitedly. "And look at this special one I made for you guys!" Beatriz held up a skull and crossbones against a crayoned violet background. "Nobody but us will get it!"

We laughed, admiring them all. "Perfect!" I said.

Then her face fell. "But I'm afraid it will rain and everything will be ruined."

"Nah," Max said. "Look—the sun's coming out. A little bit." The sun was indeed peeking from the overcast sky, the low haze drifting and dissipating. The temperature seemed to immediately shoot up.

"I gotta go. My mama and I are making *quindim* right now for the Fiesta," Beatriz said. "I'll see you later! I can't wait!"

We left Beatriz's magnificent flags in my yard and went to Max's, where Mr. Friedmann was in the kitchen washing dishes, a web punctuated with egg sacs hanging high over him. "Come back in a few minutes ven I finish and vee can pick vatermatoes for your party."

We gathered a few kitchen chairs, a couple stools, and a rusty lawn chair and stashed them in my yard. From there, we sneaked out three of my grandmother's ancestral walnut dining room chairs and a potty chair with a high, soft seat that my grandfather had used when he'd had his hemorrhoids. Luckily we didn't run into Dimma, who was probably upstairs enjoying her first Cutty and Chesterfield of the day. We crossed over to the Shreves', where we hoped Beau and D.L. might help us out, if they weren't in the mood to rough us up or play war.

"Wah, gennlmen!" Mrs. Shreve said, opening the screen

door. "How nass to see you. Ah'm afraid the boweez are at baseball practice."

"Can we borrow some chairs for the Fiesta?" I said. "Beau said you had some folding ones you take to baseball games."

"Of cawws you can, sweethot. They are raht thaya in the cahpowut—just take 'em. We are so lookin' fowud to the potty."

We spent some time arranging the furniture in our yard. Then, figuring it was time to collect the watermatoes, we went to Max's backyard, where Mr. Friedmann was fooling around in his garden. It was amazing, even in September—overrun with shiny green peppers, tomatoes, head-size cabbages, yellow squash and zucchini on hairy, contorted vines, leggy string beans still dangling from their stick teepees. Mr. Friedmann picked his way over to his eggplants, where the deep-purple fruit hung nearly to the ground, the leaves riddled with holes. "Ach, zhese lacebugs! Vhy can't you boys collect *zose*?"

Dozens of yellow cabbage butterflies danced over the squash blossoms in the hot, brightening air, indistinguishable from the small locust leaves that were falling from the trees.

"Come, boys! Zhese vatermatoes are all for you. Pick vhat you vant." In a corner of the garden, fenced off with chicken wire to keep the "warmints" from eating them, were Mr. Friedmann's watermatoes. Nobody else was able to grow them because he had a secret formula—Max told us his dad *peed* on them—to produce pretty, round fruits a little bigger than cherry tomatoes but with the wonderful taste and crisp consistency of watermelon. We thought they were miraculous, but were forbidden to pick them. Dimma said that Mr. Friedmann could get rich with his secret technique, but I don't think the Friedmanns cared about money. Giving Max a colander, Mr. Friedmann showed us the least damaging way to pick the watermatoes, saying, "And you can eat a few—it's nearly lunchtime—but leaf plenty for your party." He went in the house and returned with thick hunks of dark bread slathered with butter. "Now you don't eat so many!" Mr. Friedmann said, adding, *"Never put zhyself in the vay of temptation; even David could not resist it."*

"Aww, Pop," Max said, handing over the full colander. "Always with the Talmud."

"I'll go vash zhese and bring zhem to your party."

We were so hot we ran the hose over our heads to cool off, although I was careful not to ruin my new war paint. Then we lay in the shade of the climbing maple to rest. Looking up, we could see one or two silken lines strung horizontally between trees, which we now knew were made by "ballooning"—spiders floating on the breeze like parachutists. Gold and red maple leaves drifted down around us. "Your dad's so nice," Ivan said.

I asked Max, "Who's David?"

Max said, "You know—the shrimpy guy who killed a giant moron named Goliath with a slingshot."

"Oh, yeah," I said, remembering. "I have that in a storybook Estelle gave me. What could David not resist?"

"I forget, something with some lady?"

I wondered why Max knew so many Bible stories, so I asked.

"Almost everybody in the Bible is *Jewish,* dummy! *Jesus* was Jewish! Jews taught Christians everything they know!" Max thought for a second. "But Jews do have too many dumb rules. Sheesh."

Now I was really confused. Jesus was *Jewish*? I thought my family was Christian, and I said to Ivan, "Are you guys Christian?"

"Elena told me once that my grandfather was Jewish, back in Ukraine in the olden days. Some bad Cossack guys had a club called SMERSH, and they put him in jail till he died."

"What's a Cossack?" I asked him.

"Like a Nazi cowboy, I think."

Max whistled. "How come you never told us that?"

Ivan shrugged again.

I was realizing what a man of many secrets Ivan was, and his revelation confused me more than ever. "Are Catholics Christian?" I asked, wondering about Beatriz.

"They have that Pope guy," Max explained. "And he's like a king, and then Mary, who's like a queen, but I'm not sure about Jesus. *And* they have some secret knights who are supposed to take over the world. At least that's what I heard at Hebrew school."

I wondered if I should ask Brickie about all this news, but it might be a can of worms that didn't need opening.

Max sighed. "I hate when the leaves start to fall."

"But they're pretty," Ivan said, catching a rosy maple leaf.

"Yeah, but it's reminding me that we gotta go to school *tomorrow.*"

This was too much sad talk for me. "Maybe it's been two hours and we can decorate the cake."

"Let's go see," Ivan said.

In the Goncharoffs' kitchen, Maria gestured at the big golden cake on the counter. "Your cake es ready. You wash your hands first." She exited, leaving it to us. I really hoped that Josef wasn't around, and I knew Ivan felt the same way.

On the counter next to the cake was the bowl of blue icing we had requested, plus a flabby rubber icing bag that put me in mind of a scary device I'd seen in my grandparents' shower—not the enema contraption, but close. Max grabbed a spatula, dredged up a blob of icing, and flung it onto the cake.

"Hey," I objected. "You don't get to do it all."

Ivan put his hand into the bowl, added another blob to the cake, and smeared it around with his fingers. "We can do it faster this way." Happily, Max and I joined in.

In minutes we had iced the cake to our satisfaction. Crumbs were mixed into the icing, giving the cake a nice fuzzy look. We licked our fingers clean. From the pantry Ivan produced a Keds box full of things we'd collected to decorate our cake. The idea was that each square of cake, when cut, would feature a party favor. Onto the icing went two green army guys, one kneeling with a bazooka, one tossing a grenade. A sparkler left over from the Fourth of July. A 1943 steel penny from my blue coin folder. A couple plastic rosebuds. A bracelet of smudgy pink pop beads. Some

Cracker Jack prizes: an airplane and a tiny working jackknife the size of a paper clip. A silver Monopoly piece dog. A shark tooth I had found at the bay. A wishbone. A piece of fool's gold from Rock Creek. A Harmon Killebrew baseball card that we didn't care about because Killebrew had failed to become Rookie of the Year. A Japanese cat's-eye marble that we didn't care about because it was Japanese. Last, we scattered M&M's and sticky pink and white Good & Plenty candies between the prizes. The cake looked grand and enticing.

"I hope Elena gets the penny," I said. I was already regretting donating it to the cause but knew she'd give it back.

"I hope General de Haan bites the fool's gold and breaks his yellow Nazi teeth," Max said. "I wish we could put dog-doo inside his piece." This cracked us up, as anything about doo-doo always did.

Ivan said sternly, "Remember, the Fiesta is to make everybody be nicer to everybody. *And* we want to get in that pool."

"Okay, it'll be *nicer* if he breaks his teeth," Max said, and we laughed some more.

We were deciding whether to clean up or leave the mess for Maria, who we knew would think we did a poor job, when we heard feet on the stairs. We froze. In another moment, in a cloud of smoke, Elena whooshed in. Startled, she yelped, "Boys! What are you doing in here?" She laughed, seeming as glad to see us as we were to see her. But I noticed her face, still discolored, and the dark shadows under her eyes. I don't think I'd ever seen her without makeup.

"We meant to surprise you, not scare you!" Ivan said.

Then Elena saw the cake and exclaimed, "My goodness! It's spectacular!" She gathered us all into a hug and said, "Let me make a drink and we'll go outside. It's too hot in here."

On the porch she took her place on the swing. "I've missed my precious boys. I'm sorry I've been so busy. Did Ivan tell you I banged myself against the swing the other night? I was trying to get Rudo off me." I couldn't help but remember the sound of Josef's loud slap, but we didn't have to answer her lie because she quickly went on. "But I'll fix myself up by Fiesta time. You'll hardly notice. Is everything ready?" She let Max light her Vogue—coral—while she drew one of the green bottles from her kimono sleeve and took two Miltowns, gulping them down with her Cuba libre.

"Almost," Max said optimistically. "All we have to do now is mix up the Special Tropical Punch, set up a couple of tables, hang Beatriz's decorations, and that's it!"

"That's great! Oh, John, is that war paint on your face? Very *dramatic.*" Elena always said just the right thing. Handing her cigarette to me, she took a swig of her Cuba libre and then offered the drink to Ivan. "You worked so hard today! You deserve a puff and a sip!" We passed our rewards around. Then Elena's smile dimmed. "I must tell you boys that I won't be able to stay at the Fabulous Family Fiesta for very long," she said.

This was devastating news. "Why can't you stay?" I whined, already dizzy.

"Something's come up," she said sadly. "A prior engagement I'd forgotten about. I am so sorry, darlings." She smiled slightly and did look genuinely sorry.

"You mean you have a date," Max said accusingly, and burped.

"Yes," she said. "A date."

"Who is it?" I asked. A hot breeze came up and she looked off into a sudden flurry of falling oak leaves and rattling acorns.

Elena returned her attention to us, saying, "Oh, it's an old friend who's in town. I didn't expect him to be here so soon. He's an artist and a baseball player from Cuba."

I said, "But Cuba is *bad*."

Ivan looked crushed. "But you *are* coming to the Fiesta, right?"

"Of course I am! I just can't stay." She reached out for Ivan and hugged him, but he just went floppy in her arms. "And boys, Cuba is *not* bad. They're trying to help poor people there. Don't believe everything you hear." She sighed, rising from the swing.

Max, frustrated, let loose one of his long, loud raspberries, which brought back Elena's smile, though then she winced and gently rubbed her jaw. "Don't I hear Tim? I know you boys could use a cold treat."

Tim pulled up, grinning his usual lovesick grin, and Elena came down to the street with us, holding Ivan's hand. Tim took one look at her and the smile disappeared. "What the hell happened? Are you okay?"

Avoiding his look, she said, "Rudo made me bump my

head. I'm fine." We got plain old Popsicles, but Elena didn't want anything. "I've got my treat of choice." She offered her Cuba libre to Tim, who sipped some.

Elena went back to the house, calling, "You boys get busy! You've still got a lot to do!" Tim watched her, looking concerned, and said, "I'm going to finish my route, and then I'll be back with Popsicles for your Fiesta. You guys stay cool." The dreamy truck rolled slowly away, chiming its alluring pied-piper tune. I wanted to run up to the porch and sniff the cushion of the swing, knowing that it was faded in the places where, like a Chevy Chase Shroud of Turin, Elena's reclining hip, elbow, knee, and one heavy breast had worn the striped canvas down and smelled faintly of her. I didn't, but I had before.

It was now about three-thirty. There wasn't time to worry about Elena, or be mad about her date. Our next chore was mixing the Kool-Aid at my house. Crossing the lane, we jumped in unison when Foggy, the Andersens' dog, lunged, barking furiously, as if he hadn't seen us every single day of his vicious asshole life. "Go to hell, Foggy!" I yelled, using the strongest language I could get away with if anybody heard me. Foggy stuck his black maw through the fence, teeth bared.

"Yeah, Foggy, you moron," Max taunted. "Mr. Shreve said if you ever got loose again he was going to shoot the crap out of you." The time Foggy ate the Shreves' cat, Beau had called him a nigger, and Estelle had heard it and there was big trouble. "Unreconstructed hooligans," my grandfather had called the Shreve boys, and Beau'd had to come to our house and apologize to Estelle.

"Yeah, Ngagi," I said to Foggy. "Think about a bullet in your heart!" He tilted his head, considering this. Then he scratched his neck where there was a disgusting cluster of ticks that looked like a spoonful of lentils.

In our basement I grabbed Estelle's big five-gallon bucket, tossing the string mop aside. In the yard we squirted it with the hose and filled it up. From the kitchen I retrieved the pile of Kool-Aid packets Dimma had put out—all the flavors we'd asked for. We dumped the blueberry in first, turning the water the color of Windex, then the cherry and orange and an entire sack of sugar. I grabbed a rake leaning against a crape myrtle and stirred the punch with it.

"It's brown," Ivan said. "You said it would be a really cool color, Max, like Elena's Tropical Punch fingernail polish." He frowned.

"We can fix it," Max said. "Have you got any food coloring?" We didn't, but we did have some 7 Up and some orange TruAde in the fridge and we dumped those in. That made the punch a different brown but brighter, with bubbles. "Now it will taste more tropical because of the orange."

Ivan wasn't convinced and said, "In Mexico at fiestas there's fruit and stuff floating in the punch."

"Yeah!" Max said. "We can use some of the watermatoes for floaters!"

"No—then there won't be enough for eating." I thought for a minute. "I know! Mulberries! There's *millions*!"

We ran to the old stable in our backyard, where the branches of an ancient mulberry tree hung over the roof. Climbing up, we crawled around on the scorching shingles, loading our pockets with ripe berries. Some berries had webs or fuchsia bird-doo on them, actually a lovely color, and we wiped them gently on our shorts. We dumped the berries into the punch, where they bobbed attractively.

"Perfect!" I said. "At the last minute we'll throw in all our ice plus the snowballs we froze last winter."

Max said, "Tables."

We went to the closet where my grandmother's three bridge tables were kept. The ominous sound of tinkling ice came from the kitchen. "What are you boys up to?" Dimma came around the corner wearing Estelle's apron and looking harried. "And where are my dining room chairs?" She stood with one arm akimbo, Chesterfield at her hip, her Scotch in the other hand. "Good Lord, what is on your face?"

Ignoring the third question, I said, "We need them and some tables for the Fiesta. You said we could!"

"I did no such thing." True, but she could be forgetful and I was sometimes able to work that to my advantage.

Taking a deep drag, Dimma relented. "Oh, all right, use them. But please fold my table covers and leave them neatly in the closet." She exhaled a blue cloud sideways. Her delicate eyebrows rose doubtfully over the cat-eye glasses. She was looking me over, and I hoped she wasn't going to ask me if I was *regular* today. I quickly picked up a dusty Senators cap from the closet floor and put it on to hide my ringworm. "I'll get myself ready, and bring out Estelle's eggs and cucumber sandwiches in a bit. You boys put on some clean shirts and shoes before the party, please." She sipped some Scotch. "Apparently, most of the neighbors are coming. I hope nobody minds that I'm not putting out my good tablecloths. Lord help us if it rains." She left, muttering about missing Estelle. We threw her bridge covers and the cap back in the closet and scrammed.

Stevenson had cleared the spiderwebs from our front yard. The webs had been getting sparse, we'd noticed, full of bits of prey and trash—some were only threads with dead leaves dangling from them. Mostly eggs remained tethered in corners and nooks.

We arranged the tables and chairs again, not sure we had enough seating, but the ground seemed to be dry enough for blankets. "People will be dancing and not sitting down anyway," Ivan observed.

Looking up at the sky, Max said, "The sun's still out." The sun was actually in and out of the beautiful, cottony clouds, but mostly shining. "But is it weird that I can't hear any cicadas?"

"Nah," I said optimistically. "Maybe it's a holiday for them, too."

"Decorations!" Ivan said. With duct tape, we stuck Beatriz's arty flags up around our brick front steps, the stage for the entertainment. Ivan brought a long string of brightly colored tissue squares, and we tied those from boxwood to boxwood. Max had a pocketful of balloons that we blew up and taped to the chair backs, popping a few for the hell of it.

Then we set up my archery target out by the hedge and put our entertainment paraphernalia on the stage.

Our last task was to haul out the Kool-Aid bucket, into which we cranked the ice from every freezer tray, adding last winter's gritty snowballs. Ivan and I lugged the bucket from the kitchen to the front yard, and we hoisted it onto a table. Brickie came out with Dixie cups, paper plates, plastic forks, tons of napkins, bottle openers, and a fly swatter, saying, "I expect flies will be an issue, but try not to swat the food." Looking around, he said, "I must say, you boys have done a good job. You're to be commended!" He went back into the house and returned with his new Magnavox Holiday record player, records piled on top, and set it up on our stage. "*I'll* be in charge of the music."

"But, Brickie, make sure you play records *we* like, too, not just your jazz stuff. We want *everybody* to dance."

"Don't worry about that. There's music for all." Brickie was fairly democratic in his tastes; he also liked R&B and listened to WUST, and before Dimma put a stop to it, he used to go to places like the Bohemian Caverns to hear live music. And he loved to dance. So I wasn't too worried, but he was obsessed with his Miles Davis *Kind of Blue* record, which had just come out. Nobody normal could dance to that.

Dimma brought out two big platters, one of deviled eggs, one piled high with tiny sandwiches. "There will be no eating until after the guests have arrived and we've welcomed them," she said to us. "And everybody has their drinks." She and Brickie went back into the house.

Then Liz and Brickie returned, carrying our cooler, loaded with ice from the Esso station, beer, Cokes, and 7 Ups, and set it down by the punch station. Liz looked around appraisingly and said, "This looks pretty cool! I'm surprised you little squares pulled it off!" She and Brickie each stole an egg, poking them whole into their mouths, so we did, too. "Quality control, you understand," Brickie said. We laughed with him. As he and Liz went in to change clothes, Brickie spotted the potty chair and carried it back into the house.

We were ready for our Fabulous Family Fiesta.

First to arrive were the De Haans, the General in the lead, Madame, Kees, and Piet behind. Max stage-whispered to us, *"Oosegay eppingstay!"* My grandparents, steeling themselves, came out of the house to greet them with thin-lipped smiles. Brickie rolled his eyes at us and started up a Don Barreto record—he'd been a Don Barreto fan since his and Dimma's Havana days, when they went gambling and clubbing at the Tropicana. That they couldn't go anymore was yet another reason, in Brickie's book, for being mad about the Cuban revolution. The boys and I politely greeted the De Haans and shook hands with the General, who was actually cordial. I saw Max wipe his hand on his shorts, though. We offered them punch.

We were happy to see the Montebiancos next, all smiles. The Senhor looked fabulous in a pale-blue guayabera with white embroidery down the front, and Beatriz, carrying a bag and her hula hoop, sported her new bob with confidence. She wore her cute red skort—those were popular that year—but it didn't hide her scabby knee. Senhora carried a plate of golden pastries and was followed by Zariya, angelic in her blond bob. She clapped her hands and hugged us. Senhor toted a jug of something pale gold, and my grandfather's eyes lit up. Beatriz went to speak to Brickie and gave him a record, which made him laugh. She deposited her props on the steps with ours. Ivan told her how great her flags looked, especially the purple pirate-vinegaroon one.

The rest of the neighborhood descended on us all at once. "We've got some fun stuff," Beau Shreve shouted, brandishing a paper sack. His mother said, "You boweez behave nayow," setting down a pan loaded with pigs in a blanket. Mr. Shreve limped up on his war leg, carrying two six-packs of National Bohemian under each arm, yelling, "Yessiree, brewed on the showahs of the Chesapeake Bay!" Then came the Friedmanns, with a wooden bowl of watermatoes and a pastry box from Hofberg's. They gave the De Haans a wide berth but smiled and waved unenthusiastically to them. Mr. Friedmann spread out a worn quilt. Then came the Andersens, with a cheese plate. Liz came running out in her yellow sundress, grateful to see Maari—someone closer to her age.

The Wormy Chappaquas, a united front of grayness, offered cookies and shy smiles.

"Rats," Ivan whispered to us. "The Advice Lady!"

Taking forever to waddle up with her pathetic dog, bringing nothing but advice, she called out, "I hope you're not serving anything with mayonnaise in this heat." She shuffled over to where Dimma, Madame de Haan, and Senhora sat.

The Goncharoffs arrived, Maria bearing a platter of what looked like hundreds of diminutive tacos arranged around a generous bowl of salsa. Katya and Alexander were for once in shorts (but no shirts), and Josef was wearing a gabardine shirt and an overly big smile. He said, "A fabulous fiesta, all right!" and went to speak to the ladies, who greeted him curtly. Brickie had his eyes on him, I noticed. Where was Elena? I looked at Ivan, and he said, "She's not going to come over with *him.* She's probably bringing the cake."

Then came the Pond Lady, which really surprised us, but she had some kind of portable breathing thing. Josephine, so pretty in a turquoise lace dress, pushed her along in a wheelchair, and winked to acknowledge us. They settled in with the other ladies. Brickie played Duke Ellington's "Take the A Train."

Gellert and his family came up hesitantly, eyes darting about. We welcomed them heartily, wishing Elena was there to see how hospitable we were being, and reassured the family that Elena'd arrive soon. I pulled over two chairs for Gellert's parents, and we directed them to the drinks and food.

The adults migrated to the punch and beer table, where Max was ladling our Special Tropical Punch into Dixie cups and Senhor Montebianco was topping off each one with a generous splash from his jug. Mr. Shreve handed out beers and made boisterous remarks. My grandmother looked doubtfully into her cup and said, "I hope the rum sterilizes whatever is in here." She smiled flirtatiously at Senhor, who said, "Rum improves *all* things, *moca charmosa*." They walked off together, leaving the rum jug behind. Max quickly emptied the entire jug into the punch bucket. We helped ourselves. The grown-ups were paying no attention. It seemed possible they might be enjoying themselves. Liz begged Brickie for "The Stroll," and she lined up all the younger people, trying to teach us the very hip dance, but only she and Maari could do it.

Maria and Josephine fussed around the food tables and people began eating. The Good Humor truck came up the street, Tim clanging his bells as if it were Paris on VE day. He loped up the yard with a Thompson's Dairy ice chest, looking younger in civilian clothes. "Where's Elena?" he asked, handing out Popsicles. I said confidently, "She'll be here," although I wasn't feeling confident at all and wondered if Ivan was. Tim grabbed a beer and joined the men around the record player. He snapped the bottle open with his belt buckle, impressing my grandfather and Mr. Shreve, who said, before pushing a mayonnaise-filled deviled egg into his face, "We could use a tricky boy with your skills down at HQ. Think of the intel you could gather from an ice cream truck!"

After two cups of punch, three eggs, and many tacos, I felt languid and lay down on the thick St. Augustine grass. Ivan, Max, and Beatriz joined me. We surveyed the scene. The little kids ran wild, followed by Gellert and Zariya, who were supposedly watching them. Beau and D.L. slunk around with food in their hands, looking for opportunities to swipe beers. The General sat talking to the Pond and Advice ladies. Tim and Maria, the Andersens, and Max's mom and dad began rumba-ing, following the Montebiancos' lead, to the music of what I thought I recognized as Brickie's hero Laurindo Almeida. The other men stood together, drinking and discussing the records that lay all over the steps. People kept cheerfully helping themselves to beers or more Special Tropical Punch.

And then, finally, Elena made her appearance, looking gloriously Rosalind Russell in an off-the-shoulder white blouse, black capris, and a blue scarf, and carrying our cake. A large alligator bag hung from one shoulder. "My friends! You've made a wonderful party!" Setting down the cake on the table, she waved to the adults and made a beeline for Gellert's mom and dad. Then she made the rounds, talking with people, hugging Gellert, and after a while she came over to our spot on the grass. "I'm so glad Gellert's family came!" she exclaimed. "Thank you, my darlings!" She sat down with us, stretching out her long goddess legs. Max jumped up, wobbling a bit, and got Elena punch and cake, giving her the piece with my steel penny. Plucking it off and licking it clean, she handed it to me and said, "Keep it for me, will you, John?" Taking a sip of punch, she exclaimed, "Wow! I did need this!" and drained her cup. Max refilled it. "My face looks better, doesn't it?" she asked, and we all agreed. Kees and Piet shyly joined us, sitting on the periphery of our little group. The Shreve boys sauntered up, and I could tell they wanted to sit with us, but they stood. Elena was like the sun and we were all planets in her orbit. Blue icing around all our mouths, we cracked jokes about our parents, or, in my case, grandparents. Kees and Piet were actually funny—Kees remarked that the General won the award for Biggest Beer Gut at the party, and it would be hard for him to get close enough to anyone to dance. D.L. said his mom was such a good dancer she'd make a great stripper, which made us laugh, though we knew it was over the line. "D.L.! That's your *mother*!" Elena said, but she laughed, too. The Shreves moseyed off to steal more beer and chug it in the porte cochere.

Louis Jordan's "Reet, Petite, and Gone" was playing, and several of the older grown-ups couldn't help themselves and began jitterbugging to the irresistible tune. Brickie and Dimma were the best dancers, I noticed, although Mrs. Shreve really *was* good, and so was the Senhor. "We can dance if you want, Elena," I said, though I didn't know if I'd be able.

"Oh, I'm fine right here with you kids." Ivan moved closer, laying his head on her thigh. I was seized again with intense longing.

Tim walked over, a beer in his hand, his nice shirt translucent with sweat. "You look great, as usual," he said to Elena. "Where's this date of yours?"

Elena smiled. "He's picking me up in a little while."

"Well, please put me on your dance card before then, Miss Fabulous Family Fiesta Queen."

"Maybe when it cools off a little." She fanned herself with her hand.

"I can wait." Tim smiled and staggered off, pulling Liz, thrilled at his attention, into the circle of swinging bodies.

Beatriz said, "We should do the entertainment now that Elena's here." Although I had been excited about showing off for the guests, I felt too woozy and good to get up and do anything, let alone shoot arrows. I was afraid that now I couldn't hit the broad side of a barn.

"C'mon, you guys, get up!" Beatriz ordered.

The three of us rose reluctantly and walked a little unsteadily behind Beatriz toward our front steps. Brickie stopped the record player.

Beatriz shouted, "Attention! Attention! Ladies and gentlemen, we proudly present our entertainment! We hope you enjoy it!" Everyone moved closer to the steps and got quieter, except for the Shreve boys, who yelled, "Oh, *no*! Circus acts!"

Mrs. Shreve hissed at them, "*Hush,* you wrayetches."

We stood there stupidly, and Max whispered, "Who's going first?"

Ivan and I shook our heads and Beatriz said, "I'm going *last* because I'm the main attraction."

"Okay, you chickens," Max said. "I guess I'll just get this over with." He picked up his glittery new Duncan Imperial and spun it out a couple times to warm up. He Walked the Dog, receiving some applause, then followed that with a Skin the Cat, a Sleeper, and an Around the World, all perfectly executed in quick succession. He bowed, and everyone applauded, and Tim gave an ear-splitting whistle.

Next, Ivan stepped up to do his magic tricks. Josef shouted, "Here comes Houdini!" but Ivan didn't look his way.

Red-faced, he said, "I dedicate this performance to my aunt Elena, because she's magic!"

First Ivan did a kind of dopey trick where he unbent a spoon with his mind—first strenuously miming bending it, then pretending to unbend it, dramatically showing the intact spoon. "Wow! Great!" the crowd called out politely. Then he did the Magic Coloring Book, where he showed the audience an uncolored book by flipping through its pages, then gave a magical flourish, and showed it again, fully colored. More enthusiasm for that one. Finally, his pièce de résistance. Bringing out four shiny rings, he demonstrated that they were unconnected, with no gaps, and he proceeded to fiddle with them, forming first a chain of four—cries of amazement—then a four-leaf clover. There was delighted clapping and calls for more. Tim whistled again. But Ivan only bowed and waved to Elena and ran to the back of the crowd to nestle beside her.

I felt a bit heartened by all the enthusiasm so far, but for a moment I seriously considered going into the house and hiding under my bed. But I saw Beau and D.L. smirking off to the side, then I looked at Brickie, and he nodded solemnly, giving me a thumbs-up. Elena knew I was faltering and blew me a kiss. I resolved not to disappoint them. Picking up my bow and an arrow, I yelled, "Everybody has to move away from the target!" The target was not very far, close to the street, behind the crowd, but I felt like it was a hundred miles away. The crowd parted. I drew back on my bow, setting my feet apart, trying to steady myself, and let the arrow go. It hit an inner circle, not the bull's-eye, but not a disgrace, either. There was some clapping. I drew back on another arrow, but as I did, I spied the satanic Schwinn on the lane behind the crowd, nearly obscured by the hedge. Nobody but Max, Beatriz, and I, high on the stage facing the lane, could really see it. Max hissed, *"Slutcheon!"* The bike approached our yard. Either it was too late for me to stop or the Special Tropical Punch gave me a jolt of courage, or insanity. Aiming just to the left of the big target, I let my arrow fly, and it landed in the spokes of Slutcheon's front wheel. He wobbled crazily for a second, trying to stay on the bike, but then ditched on his side. He scrambled up fast, his nasty face looking stunned. He limped and remounted, and kept going. Incredibly, he didn't scream anything, and more incredibly, I guess because of the punch or because I was up higher, the grown-ups hadn't noticed what transpired behind the hedge, just that I'd been seriously off target. There were calls of "Aww!" and "That's okay! Try again!" But Max, Beatriz, and the Shreve boys, who'd been watching from the branches of a dogwood, all clapped and whooped ecstatically. Max hollered, "Go, Johnny, go!" I couldn't believe what I'd done and knew there'd be hell to pay with Slutcheon, but I didn't care. I readied my last arrow. Feeling brave and rock-solid now, I shot again. The arrow hit the target to the right of the first one, barely inside the center circle, but definitely a bull's-eye. The crowd hollered, "Bravo!" and "William Tell!" and best of all, there was a shout of "Just like Errol Flynn!" I knew it was Brickie who'd yelled it, but that was fine. Elena and Ivan grinned and waved. I gave a Robin Hood–like bow, wishing I'd worn my old Peter Pan cap with its hawk feather, which would have added the perfect flourish.

Beatriz stepped up, now wearing a grass skirt over her skort and holding her hula hoop, announcing, "And now, in honor of Hawaii, our new fiftieth state, I will perform to the song 'Me Rock-a-Hula,' by Mr. Bill Haley and His Comets." I couldn't help thinking that if she still had her long hair she would look more Hawaiian, but she was an eyeful. Max was agog.

Brickie put her record on, and she began swiveling her hips, hula-hooping *and* hula-dancing in perfect time to the rocking music. Everybody clapped along. She hula-ed all over the stage, and then came down the steps, into the audience, still performing her spectacular moves, until the song was over. The crowd went wild. Max let out some wolf whistles, and Tim shouted, "Well, A-lo-HA, Miss Hawaii!" She curtsied several times as her mom, dad, and sister called out, "Brava! Brava!" Gellert ran up, grinning, and sniffed Beatriz's hair appreciatively. The De Haans came over to congratulate us and tell us how much they were enjoying the Fiesta, the General telling Max, "I vas goodt vit a yo-yo vhen I vas a boy. I should show you zome tricks. Come over vun day and I vill!" Josephine moseyed over and said, "I'm sho glad to see you kids doin' something *constructive.* And in the *daytime.*" Then she gave us each a hug, spilling a little of her beer on Max, who didn't care a bit, he was so happy.

Brickie put on the Jackie Wilson "Reet Petite" that we kids loved, and I cried, "Let's dance, Beatriz!" She and I joined the dancers and began bopping. Beatriz was good at it and I was lousy, but Beatriz didn't mind. Everyone belted out the refrain, *"Uh oh oh oh, uh oh oh oh."* Max tapped me on the shoulder. I backed off, incredulous, and Max and Beatriz danced. All the grown-ups—at least those who could—were whirling and laughing, and, except for the Chappaquas, not with their spouses, I noticed: Dimma and Senhor, Brickie and Mrs. Shreve, Mrs. Friedmann and Josef, Mr. Friedmann and Josephine, the General and Mrs. Andersen, Tim and Maria, and Madame with Mr. Shreve, who was doing pretty well with his game leg. Beau and D.L. were dancing with Maari and Liz! Gellert danced with Zariya! Even the toddler tribe goofily rocked out. "The Beaver Plan is working!" I hollered at Ivan. Even the Pond and Advice ladies, parked off to the side, seemed to be having fun, although the Advice Lady couldn't resist calling, "You people are going to *expire* in this heat," as if the guests were deviled eggs, but it was true that everyone was shiny with sweat. Ivan and I dragged Elena up, and she danced with us both, giving us extra twirls. But then Tim broke in and he and Elena bopped. Ivan and I jigged around together—who cared if we were both boys. The Senhora begged off from Mr. Andersen, probably to keep a better eye on Beatriz, or the Senhor, so Mr. Andersen began dancing with me and Ivan, which was a little disturbing, and in a few moments we sat down. He didn't seem to mind and continued a sort of interpretive dance with Kees and Piet.

To cool things down, Brickie played one slow, dreamy

song after the other—"You Send Me," the Platters' "Smoke Gets in Your Eyes," "Mona Lisa." He claimed Elena with an eager smile, and all the dancers clung together, seemingly in slow motion and love, swaying to the romantic songs. Watching, I felt like Ivan and I had become the square adults, chaperoning teenagers at a sock hop. The toddlers, Zariya, and Gellert threw themselves down on a blanket clutching their cake prizes, faces stained with Popsicles and blue icing, and passed out. Tim was now dancing with *both* Maari and Liz in a clumsy bear hug.

Elena plopped back down with us. "I believe it is a successful Fabulous Family Fiesta," she said softly. "Maybe you boys will win the Nobel Peace Prize." We were paralyzed with happiness and rum, so glad her date hadn't come. Max and Beatriz returned, and we all drew nearer to Elena. She bent over Ivan, hugging him to her, whispering in his ear, and gave him something that he pocketed. She checked her watch again.

Darkness wasn't far off. The light was gloamy and otherworldly, the grass and trees an incandescent green, the tall clouds the luscious pastel of orange Creamsicles. The opening strains of "The Twelfth of Never" floated out into the hot and surreally still evening air, Johnny Mathis's honeyed voice putting us all in a sweaty reverie. "Oh, this *song*!" cried Elena. "Listen!" She began singing along.

You ask how much I need you, must I explain?
I need you, oh, my darling, like roses need rain

You ask how long I'll love you; I'll tell you true:
Until the Twelfth of Never, I'll still be loving you

Tears welled up in Elena's eyes, but she laughed at the schmaltzy moment as she sang the refrain.

Hold me close, never let me go
Hold me close, melt my heart like April snow

"Isn't it just the *loveliest* song?"

Max just *had* to say, though apologetically, "It's kind of corny, Elena." She laughed again, wiping her eyes. Ivan looked like he might cry, or throw up, but he did neither, snuggling against her. I wanted to, too. Elena kept singing, rocking slightly from side to side with her big baby.

Then things began to happen fast. From down the lane came the roar of something that wasn't a car. The boys and I rose to our knees to see what it was. A man on a motorcycle big as a pony pulled up at the Goncharoffs' gate and idled there. The rider had long, curly hair and a scraggly beard that managed not to obscure his handsome face. Despite the heat, the man wore a green military jacket and heavy boots. The dancers stopped, all eyes on the street.

"Damn," Tim said, coming forward. "Not a *beatnik*." The man spotted Elena, lifting his bearded chin to acknowledge her.

Elena stood, shouldering her big bag, and said, "Goodbye, my precious darlings." She kissed us all, then whispered again to Ivan, who looked stricken. She walked quickly across the lawn. At the street, she climbed onto the back of the motorcycle, calling out, "Thank you for a lovely party!"

Max said darkly, "That's not a baseball player."

Mr. Shreve turned to my grandfather and said loudly, "Jesus Christ, is that *Camilo*?"

"I'm afraid it might be," said Brickie, his face as grim as I'd ever seen it. "You'd better call in."

Josef strode across the lawn, his face twisted and red, shouting in Spanish, but the man gunned his engine, laughing. *"Vas bien, Fidel!"* he called. He and Elena roared off. Josef hurled a beer bottle that smashed explosively in the street.

"You barbudos bastard!" Mr. Shreve yelled, fiddling with the walkie-talkie thing on his belt. Elena did not look back, but raised a hand and waved slowly, like Queen Elizabeth at her coronation. Her scarf blew off, and her hair whipped wildly around her.

For a moment there was only Johnny Mathis. The neighbors stood silently, confused and stunned, not having any idea what was happening, but understanding that it was something terrible. The Andersens and the Chappaquas said their goodbyes and rushed off.

Then a deafening boom rattled my bones, followed by a huge flash. Then staccato blasts. "Gunfire!" yelled Tim. Everybody shrieked.

Max screamed, "A mushroom cloud! A mushroom cloud!" We all looked up. Above the trees loomed an enormous thunderhead, its double anvil shape roiling toward us, now glowing a radioactive pink in the dying sun. More blasts.

There was a babble of languages and shouts of "God help us!" "Run!" The music stopped with a painful, ripping screech.

I shouted, "Duck and cover!" and we three scrambled under the tables, peeking out fearfully. More blasts went off. Ivan cried, and Beatriz was crying as she and her parents gathered Zariya and ran down the lane. Mr. Friedmann called out, "Max! Max! Come home!" and he and Mrs. Friedmann stumbled off. Gellert's family hurried away. Dimma and Josephine struggled to get the Pond Lady and the Advice Lady into the house, the Advice Lady squawking, "I knew this day would come! We're all doomed!" Tim's truck zoomed off, and Maria grabbed the twins and ran across the lane. There was another hair-raising crack, another flash, and rain began pouring down. The air went dark and biblical. The General stood on the steps, calling out, *"Mijn God! Het is als Rotterdam 1940!"* and lurched off with his family. Brickie shoved his Magnavox inside the door, yelling, "Stay calm! It's not a bomb! It's just a storm! Everyone stay calm!" but by then almost everybody was gone. Mr. Shreve and Josef stood out in the lane in the deluge, Josef still in a rage, Mr. Shreve using his walkie-talkie. Mr. Shreve went home, leaving Josef, soaked, looking like a horror-movie maniac, clutching Elena's blue scarf in one hand, the other clutching his heart.

Thunder boomed again, but farther off. More lightning. We crawled out from under the table, splattered with spilled salsa. From around the back of our house came Beau and D.L., running backward toward home, throwing one more cherry bomb and laughing hysterically. D.L. shouted, "Ha ha! We got your Harmon Killebrew card, too!"

Liz was trying to carry food platters inside. *"God!"* she shrieked. "It was those hick morons with their cherry bombs!" She stomped into the house. We stood in the downpour and flashes—I wasn't even thinking about black lightning, only Elena.

Ivan still cried, looking off down the lane where Elena had disappeared. Brickie stuck his head out the door and said, "You boys break it up now. Time to be home—you have school tomorrow." I went straight to bed in my damp, dirty clothes. I guess Dimma was too drunk, or too busy dealing with the old ladies, to make me bathe and change.

13

I woke up with a headache, sweat soaking my sheets. The day was overcast, but I could tell by the heat that it was not early. Why hadn't anybody gotten me up for school? The house seemed oddly quiet, no sounds coming up from the kitchen or my grandparents' room. Maybe Dimma and Brickie were still drunk. I lay there for a moment, thinking about the night before: the Fiesta, the great music and dancing, Elena riding off on the motorcycle, the crazy, apocalyptic conclusion to the party, and whether any of it meant anything new. I heard noise from the street, adults talking, and car doors slamming, and guessed that maybe the grown-ups were out there cleaning up the party mess, which was supposed to be our job after school.

When I went to the open window, I saw groups of adults—Brickie and Mr. Shreve among them—standing in front of the Goncharoffs'. A police car and an ambulance idled in the street. My heart clenched. Up and down Connors Lane, neighbors stood silently in their yards, staring. The Goncharoffs' front door gaped, but I couldn't see any of the family. I didn't see Max or Ivan, who I knew normally would be rubbernecking at any event involving emergency vehicles. I ran down the stairs and out into our front yard, where the Fiesta dishes and our decorations lay trashed and sodden. Dimma's precious walnut chairs were black from the rain, and she stood in her housecoat, hugging herself as if she were freezing. She grabbed me as I tried to run past her, falling to a crouch with her arms around me. I thought I was about to get spanked because of the ruined chairs, and I struggled to get away. "John! John, look at me, sweetheart," she said. I stopped, frozen with dread, and she held both my arms tightly.

"What's wrong? What's wrong?" I cried. "Dimma, what's going on?"

Dimma said, "Something terrible happened last night, John." Her voice trembled, something I'd never heard before, and that alarmed me even more. "Your friend Elena died last night."

A strangled, desperate laugh came from my throat. "You're joking, Dimma!" But Dimma's face was contorted with sadness, and tears filled her eyes. She held me tighter and kissed me. "My poor, sweet boy," she whispered.

"No she didn't! No she didn't!" Using every ounce of my strength I broke away from Dimma, hurtling toward the street.

Dimma, weeping now, called, "John! Come back! Please stay here! There's nothing you can do."

I ran past the adults, and Brickie, who tried to grab me, to Ivan's house, calling, "Ivan! Ivan!" Halting on the porch, I looked wildly around for Ivan or Elena. There, huddled on the floor against the wall, I saw my friends. Max, sniffling, had his arm around Ivan, whose dirty, tearstained face was white with what? Fear? Horror? "It's not true, is it? It's not true! *Say it's not true!*" Max looked at me miserably but said nothing. Ivan stared off, shaking uncontrollably. "What happened? *What happened to her?* Did . . . did he . . . hurt her?"

Ivan looked at me then and said wonderingly, "She . . . she sat in The Throne. Why'd she *do* that?" and began sobbing. I wanted to shout out, *"How could he kill her for that?"* But I could only collapse next to Ivan, hugging him tightly. I began crying, too. We stayed that way for what seemed a long time. Nobody bothered us; the men were busy talking to one another and to the police, writing things, doing things. The neighbor ladies—Mrs. Friedmann, Mrs. Shreve, La Senhora—stood shocked and teary-eyed in the lane. I thought I could hear, way back somewhere in the house, Maria's weeping.

The ambulance drove off, and I understood then that inside it was our darling Elena. Max, watching the ambulance, began softly humming "Taps," but he couldn't get past the *"gone the sun"* part before the dirge choked in his throat. A policeman and a man in a jacket and tie came onto the porch and they began winding yellow tape around the railings, closing the area off. The cop went into the house. Before following him, the other man spoke kindly to Ivan, and said that he was a detective. Then he told us not to touch anything. "We haven't had a chance to examine the scene yet." He said that Ivan should go inside—this made me shudder—and Max and I should go home and be with our families. But we weren't going anywhere unless we went together.

Brickie came up onto the porch and went into the house for a moment. He came back and squatted down with us. "Why don't you boys all come over to our house for now? We'll get you some breakfast, you can watch TV, and things might seem a little . . . more normal. There certainly won't be any school today." Brickie reached out to Ivan and took his hand, gently pulling him up. "We'll just take it easy, okay? Ivan, I told your dad you were coming with us." He hugged Ivan to his side. "Try not to worry, son. Not right now. Let's just get through the day." As they walked to the lane, the neighbors began drifting off, stopping to give Ivan hugs, which he silently tolerated.

Max and I stood to follow. Max, catching up to Ivan and Brickie, threw his arm around Ivan protectively. Coming behind them, I glanced at The Throne with a mixture of feelings—I wanted to either burn it down or make it into some kind of shrine to Elena—where she last had been our living, loving, laughing goddess. Then I spotted something jammed back in its cushions. Glancing around to make sure nobody was watching, I hurried over, and from the cushions I pulled out Ivan's green prescription bottle, marked with the skull and crossbones. It was empty and the cap was gone. A paralyzing sense of alarm came over me. I guessed that nobody had seen it yet because it was well camouflaged by the green foliage print of the upholstery. Sniffing it, I detected the faint odor of vinegar. I shivered, the hair on my arms and neck standing up, but I couldn't think and just pocketed the bottle. Catching up to Brickie and the boys, I turned, checking again to see if anyone had come out of the house and seen me. There was no one, only Elena's swing slowly drifting forward and back, forward and back.

Brickie and Dimma fixed Ivan and me a big breakfast: scrambled eggs, bacon *and* sausage patties, buttered toast, chocolate milk, and orange juice. Max's parents had made him come home to go to school. Ivan hardly touched a thing on his plate, and Brickie said, "Ivan, try to eat something. You need to keep up your strength." Ivan didn't reply, but he finally ate a piece of toast and drank some chocolate milk. I didn't have much of an appetite, either, and Brickie for once didn't badger me. He and Dimma sat at the table and chatted pleasantly to each other, which I knew was fake because Dimma was rarely downstairs so early and they didn't talk much in the morning anyway. Estelle arrived, and she must have heard what had happened from the neighbors, because before she even set her purse down, she came over to Ivan and rubbed his head, hugged him, and said, "Poor little fella. God bless you, baby." Then she hugged me, too. I was dazed, haunted by what was in my pocket. After a while, I said, "May we be excused?" and Dimma allowed us to take our chocolate milk into the living room to watch TV.

I turned on *Looney Tunes.* Ivan and I sat close to each other and stared at the screen. I wanted to talk to Ivan, but more than that I wanted Ivan to talk to *me.* Finally, I reached into my pocket for the green pill bottle. I held it out. Ivan looked at it, and then looked at me, his red-rimmed blue eyes filling with tears. "Ivan, what happened to the vinegaroon?"

He put a hand in his pocket and drew out the cap. After a second, he said, "He must have got away."

"What do you mean, *got away*? How?"

"Why did she have to sit on his Throne?" He began crying a little bit.

"I don't know," I said. Then, petrified, I asked, "Did you put the vinegaroon there?"

"It wasn't for her!" he wailed. "I didn't mean for it to bite *her*! When I was going to bed, I heard someone walking around, and I thought it was . . . *him,* and that he'd go out to smoke his cigar, so I snuck down to the porch and put it in The Throne for *him.* But *she* sat there! She told me at the Fiesta that she wasn't coming home—she had to get away from him, but she'd come back for me soon." He blubbered, "I just wanted to *hurt* him, not kill him. I *think.*"

I was speechless for a moment with horrified comprehension. Then I asked, "Nobody knew about the vinegaroon but us, right?" I took the cap from him and put that and the pill bottle in my pocket. I tried to think, but I wanted to cry.

"It'll be okay, Ivan," I said, although I knew it wouldn't be. "It was an accident. We're just little boys." But what I felt was that we were something else now, yawing away from our innocent earthly lives, a dark unknown before us.

"We have to go bury the bottle, okay?"

"Okay." He wiped snot and tears from his face with his T-shirt.

With new alarm I realized that the vinegaroon might still be on Ivan's porch, or in his yard somewhere, and could bite somebody else. We needed to go over to the Goncharoffs' and find him, but the police were surely still there. Not to mention Josef.

"Please don't cry, Ivan," I said. "Let's drink our milk, and then maybe we can go look for him. I bet he's hiding under some rocks, and he won't come out in the day. Nobody knows about him. But we've got to find him." It dawned on me that if the police found the vinegaroon, the Heist would be exposed as well.

Our doorbell rang, and Brickie went to open it. The cop and the detective who'd spoken to us on the Goncharoffs' porch came in. They began talking softly with Brickie, but I couldn't hear what they said, and tried to ignore them. Brickie ushered the men into the living room and introduced them, and I jumped up to shake their hands, hoping they'd think we were good boys. Ivan just stared at the TV, but he had a good excuse for forgetting his manners. "They'd like to talk to you boys for a few minutes," Brickie said.

"Okay." I prayed that Ivan wouldn't fall apart.

The detective said to him, "I'm so sorry for your loss, son. I know you were very close to your aunt." Ivan tried to smile a little. "We just want to understand what happened to her. Did you know about her asthma?"

"Yes, sir."

"Have you seen her have an attack?"

"Yeah. Lots of times."

"What did she do when she had one of these attacks?" He was writing things down.

"She . . . she coughed a lot. She had an inhaler," Ivan said. "And some pills."

"Do you know what kind of pills she had? Do you know if she had the pills and inhaler with her last night?"

Ivan thought. "No. But she usually had that stuff in the sleeve of her robe." The detective nodded, scribbling.

I spoke up. "The pills were Miltowns. All ladies have them."

"Okay," the detective said, suppressing a smile. He looked to the policeman.

The cop asked, "Do you know anything about the bruises on her face and arm?"

Ivan and I looked at each other. It suddenly came to me that if Ivan incriminated Josef, and Josef went to jail, what would happen to Ivan? Had Ivan thought of that?

Ivan said hesitantly, "Yeah, she told us she hit her face on the swing. Last week. She said one of our dogs jumped up on the swing and made it happen."

"Okay. Do you think there might be anyone who'd want to harm your aunt?"

In a rush I said, "There's a kid we call Slutcheon. He didn't like her because she was helping refugees, and some of them lived in his neighborhood, on Quincy Street, and his dad wanted to get rid of them." Here Brickie's eyebrows went up.

Ivan nodded, adding, "The girl next door hates her because her boyfriend has a crush on her."

The detective, scribbling, asked, "Do you know anything about any of the men your aunt dated? How about the guy who picked her up on a motorcycle yesterday at the party?"

"I never saw him before, I don't think," Ivan said. "Sometimes when she came home with guys, I was asleep, or it was too dark to see who they were." Then, to my horror, he blurted out, "Sometimes she got into fights with my father."

The detective looked interested. "Some of the neighbors have mentioned that. But would you say that these . . . fights were anything other than sort of normal family arguments?"

"He . . . he might have slapped her," Ivan said. "He didn't like her dates, but I'm not sure why."

"Okay." The detective wrote that down. "I think that's about it. Thank you, boys." He put his notepad in a back pocket. The men went to the door with Brickie, where they talked for another minute and left.

My grandfather came back to us and asked, "You boys all right?" We nodded. Brickie looked at us for a long moment. "Okay. We can talk about this later. As you were, then."

When he was gone, I cried, "You shouldn't have said anything about Josef!"

"He said the neighbors told him anyway. And he *deserves* to go to jail."

"But Ivan, if your dad goes to jail, what will happen to *you*?"

He thought, then shrugged. "I guess I'll go to an orphanage. Who cares, as long as I'm away from *him*."

I was still very concerned about the missing vinegaroon, but more cars had arrived at the Goncharoffs', so we had to wait. Estelle surprised us with potato-chip sandwiches and Cokes. "Don't be gettin' the idea that you boys gonna get these from *me* again," she said. They were especially delicious, a little spicy, and she told us that she'd put some crumbled bacon and a splash of Tabasco in the Miracle Whip, "Give it a little pep, don't y'all think?" She gave Ivan's burr head another affectionate rub. "I hear yo party was a great success. I'm proud o' you boys."

I said bleakly, "It was fun. But now everything's ruined."

"Well, we cain't always understand God's 'tentions, but you boys gone be all right."

Ivan ate his whole sandwich. Exhausted, we fell asleep on the sofa for a short while. When I woke, I felt normal until I remembered everything. Ivan was already awake and said, "I hoped I'd wake up and it'd all be just a nightmare."

"Yeah. Me, too."

The pill bottle felt like it was the size of a Coke in my pocket, and a strong sense of purpose took hold of me. "We can't look for the vinegaroon yet, but we've *got* to go bury the pill bottle," I said firmly. "Right now."

We passed through the kitchen, where Dimma was sitting, doing her crossword puzzle. She looked up and said, blowing some Chesterfield smoke sideways, "Did you have a nice nap? I know you both needed one." She smiled gently at Ivan. "Wasn't that sweet of Estelle to fix your favorite sandwiches?" He nodded.

"We're going to dig up some worms. Max's snake needs them," I said.

We headed out the kitchen door to the backyard and looked around. "Let's bury it in the fountain." My mother's Lady of the Lake looked extra sad without any petunias, and I thought of my mother, and whether she'd understand what we were doing, and what we'd done. I got a shovel from the basement and began digging, going deep into the grass and dirt, soft after yesterday's wild rainstorm. Ivan sat on the flagstones around the old pond and watched blankly. After digging down about two feet, I pulled out the green pill bottle, capped it, and threw it into its grave.

As I began filling in the hole, Max appeared, home from school. He looked anxiously at Ivan, and went and sat with him. "I brought you this." He handed Ivan the new *Flash* comic book. Ivan smiled and thanked him but didn't open it.

"What are you guys doing?"

I took a big breath and answered, "The vinegaroon got out on Ivan's porch last night, and we're burying his pill bottle because it smelled like vinegar and we don't want anybody to know we stole it." I hated to have to give words to the awful story. I stopped what I was doing, leaning on the shovel like a gravedigger. Max looked from one of us to the other, trying to digest this.

He asked, "So why didn't Ivan tell me this morning? Where is the vinegaroon?"

"Ivan didn't tell you this morning because he was too upset, and I didn't know what happened." I went on. "He put the open pill bottle there for *Josef,* not for *her.*" I could not say her name. "We don't know where the vinegaroon is now, but we've got to find it before it gets someone else. And so nobody will know we stole it. But there're too many people at Ivan's house." I wasn't sure Ivan was even listening; he was looking off in the distance as if he were a million miles away.

Max's jaw fell open. After this had sunk in, he said, "You . . . you mean . . ." He was too stunned to go on.

"That's the story," I said.

Max's face grew pale. I resumed filling in the hole, and when I was done, Max came over and picked up hunks of dug-up grass and neatly placed them on top. He tamped it all down with his Chucks. Then he said, "I just thought of something. When I was coming over, I saw Rudo in Ivan's yard. He was barking and scrabbling at the ground in front of the porch. Maybe it was the vinegaroon?"

This got Ivan's attention. "Oh, *no*! He might try to eat it!"

Brandishing the shovel, we sped around front, where I saw that the cars at the Goncharoffs' were gone. But below the porch, there was Rudo, doing exactly what Max described, and, more frightening, the twins were with him, crazed putti dancing and giggling, encouraging his frenzy. Max shouted, "Ivan! Get the twins away! I'll get Rudo!"

Ivan ran to the twins and wrestled them away. Max yelled, "Rudo, NO!" He grabbed Rudo by his collar and dragged him off, holding him at a distance. Ivan screeched at the twins in Spanish, and they ran into the house. Then he and I tentatively approached the spot where Rudo had been digging. There were some loose chunks of concrete walk, but nothing else. "Please don't let Rudo have eaten him," Ivan prayed. Using the tip of the shovel, I very slowly lifted a piece of concrete. Nothing. I tried a bigger chunk, levered it up, and jumped back. "Gah! There he is!" The vinegaroon waved his claws at us and poised his whiptail. Before he could spray me, I had the big piece of concrete in my hands and hurled it down on top of him. It landed with a thud on the damp dirt. For a moment we stood silently, relieved about our rescue and the end of the vinegaroon. Then I slowly lifted the chunk again. He was completely crushed, a mass of brittle purple carapace and gluey insides, smelling of vinegar. I scooped him up with the shovel, saying, "We can't bury him because Wiesie or the dogs might dig him up. I say we burn him." Ivan took Rudo from Max, and, quietly opening the screen door, pushed him inside. We carried the vinegaroon off to my house.

Down at the stone fireplace at the end of my yard, we made a small pyre with dry leaves and sticks. I shoveled the vinegaroon, our hard-won trophy, onto the pyre and Max lit it. It burned slowly and smokily. Max said, "Too bad you didn't get a crack at Slutcheon, old buddy."

Ivan addressed the fire pitifully. "It wasn't your fault, it was mine. You were just doing your job."

"Ivan! Ivan!" Beatriz called, running down to us in her uniform. She ran straight to Ivan, throwing herself at him so forcefully that they fell down together. "Ivan! I'm so sorry! I thought about you all day!" Lying on top of him, she began crying. They struggled up, and Beatriz said, "Don't worry, we're going to take care of you!" Ivan, embarrassed, gave her a thin smile.

She wiped her eyes and asked, "What are you burning?"

"It's the vinegaroon," I said.

Beatriz looked astonished. *"Why?"*

"We need to tell her everything," Max said solemnly.

"Well, *you* can," I said. "Ivan and I don't want to hear it again." Max took Beatriz by the hand, leading her away. They stood together as Max explained our awful secret. Beatriz covered her face, sobbing. Max awkwardly put his arms around her, letting her cry. I'd never seen so much crying in all my eight years.

I said to Ivan, "Gimme your knife." I took it and swiftly drew the little blade across my wrist. Then Ivan did the same. After a second, drops of blood appeared on our cuts. "You guys come here!" I called to Beatriz and Max. Beatriz was startled when she saw the blood, but I said, "We have to swear on our secret." Max made his cut, then Beatriz, and we rubbed our wrists on one another's, our blood mixing inextricably and for all time. It was a rite the boys and I had performed before, only with tiny pricks from fingertips, and not about so enormous a secret. We were trapped in a sticky spiderweb of lies, but it felt better knowing that the four of us were in the web together.

—

From the house, I brought Band-Aids. Beatriz had to go home. The boys and I went inside and watched more TV—*The Mickey Mouse Club.* We thought we were too old for it, but who cared. Then Mrs. Friedmann came to collect Max, carrying a warm loaf of challah. She gave Ivan a bosomy hug and said, "Dear Ivan, you don't belieff zis now, but vun day life vill be goodt again."

Dimma came from the kitchen. "Ivan, we've arranged with your father for you to stay with us the rest of this week. Maria will bring over the things you need, and you two will go back to school in the morning, all right? That might be best until things settle down."

Ivan said simply, "Thanks."

"Ivan, sweetheart, things will get better, I promise."

"Okay," Ivan said. I knew he didn't believe any of it.

14

After school a couple days later, Ivan and Max and I went to Blessed Sacrament for a service for Elena. A kind young nun who had done volunteer work with Elena on refugee problems had arranged the service. Josef had had Elena cremated, so there was no casket, just flowers. The Friedmanns, the Montebiancos, and Mr. and Mrs. Shreve were there, although their boys were "under house arrayest," as Mrs. Shreve put it, because of the cherry-bomb debacle at the Fiesta. Beatriz's parents let her sit with me and Max and Ivan, and Beatriz kissed Ivan's cheek. Maria sat in the front row with Josef, weeping quietly. Tim was there, looking very handsome in a blazer and tie. He waved to us miserably. I was surprised not to see Gellert and his family.

I don't remember much of what took place: some mumbo-jumbo and church songs, a man from the refugee organization said a few words. Before long we were back at my house, where Dimma had offered to host a small wake. The adults drank coffee and a little sherry, talking quietly and nibbling what Dimma had put out—the neighbors had all brought things. None of this was very real to me, and it didn't seem to have much to do with the Elena we knew. Why weren't we all drinking Cuba libres, smoking Vogues, laughing, wearing silky kimonos, listening to "The Twelfth of Never"? *That* would have been a more fitting goodbye for her, as far as I was concerned.

Beatriz and the boys and I went out to our front steps and sat quietly, surrounded by the mournful drone of the cicadas. I thought about us being right where we were, performing at the Fiesta; it had been only days but seemed like weeks.

I noticed Ivan was twiddling a golden ring with three diamonds on his middle finger. "What's that?" I asked.

"It belonged to her grandmother," he said. "She gave it to me at the Fiesta. He doesn't know I have it. I'm gonna keep it *forever.*"

Beatriz leaned in to see. "It's so beautiful! Ivan, she's with the angels, and she's okay."

Max retorted, his mouth full of a muffin he'd eaten in one bite, "Shalami, shalami, baloney! Shee'sh gone and ish jusht dusht an' ashes now."

Ivan didn't appear to be paying much attention, but then he said, "There *might* be angels. We don't know everything. Maybe people believe in angels so they aren't scared, and dying doesn't seem so bad." He put the ring in his pocket.

"Maybe God is punishing *us* for . . . *our sins.*" Beatriz's lower lip trembled. "Like the Heist."

"But why would God punish *her*?" I asked, still not able to say *Elena*.

"Maybe God is a *moron,*" Max said, shocking Beatriz, who cried, "Don't say that, Max!"

"Everybody gets to think what they want, okay?" I said, putting an end to it.

Then the grown-ups left all at once, saying comforting things to Ivan. Josef cursorily said, "Be good, son," and patted Ivan's shoulder, but Ivan shrugged his father away. The irony of Josef telling anyone to *be good* was not lost on us—our bitterness was palpable, as if steam were coming off our heads. But what could we say?

Beatriz's parents came to take her away, and she said, "See you later. I love you guys." She blew us a kiss.

Brickie came out. "Everybody okay?"

I said, "Uh-huh. We're just out here being *stoic*."

"Is this a good time to talk about things? Ivan?"

"I don't care," he replied.

Sitting down with us, Brickie began, "I think you all need to know what's going on." He sounded so official. "The authorities have interviewed all the . . . persons of interest, and have concluded that Elena died from a severe asthma attack. She had her pills, but not her inhaler, apparently. She'd had a lot to drink, and there were traces of other injurious and unusual substances in her system that they couldn't identify—possibly other drugs. But it doesn't appear to have been . . . homicide."

Confused, Max asked, "What do you mean, 'unusual substances'? They thought she might have been *poisoned*?"

Brickie paused. Then he explained, "Elena consorted—kept company—with some individuals who didn't have her best interests at heart."

"I still don't get it," I said. "Like who?"

For a minute, Brickie looked away. "I do not know," he said stiffly, adding, "but, as I say, homicide has been ruled out. And they don't believe it was suicide, either. Maybe you boys have been worrying about that."

"Suicide?" I asked. "You mean, like she *killed* herself?" Why would Elena have done such a thing? I couldn't imagine anyone thinking Elena, so full of life, would have done that.

"Correct. The prescription bottle in the bag she was carrying still had pills, and if she'd intended to do away with herself, she likely would have taken all of those. She also had a spider bite, and there were traces of a spider-borne toxin in her system."

At this, my heart began banging in my chest. Brickie was waiting for us to say something, but I knew we were all too afraid to speak.

Brickie continued. "But Josef said she wasn't allergic to any insects, and the pathologist said that right now, of course, they're seeing many people with traces of spider toxins in their blood. A bite from a regular spider wouldn't kill anybody. It just seems to have been a combination of things, and bad luck. If she'd had her inhaler, it might not have happened. I'm truly sorry to tell you all this, Ivan. But I want you to understand. It was just a tragic accident." I could hear us each exhaling.

I badly wanted Brickie to shut up and go away, but he had more to say. "And I might as well give you *all* the bad news. Your friend Gellert and his family have to leave the country. Someone determined that they were undesirable aliens, possibly Communist sympathizers posing as refugees, but I'm not convinced of that myself. I think someone had it in for them. But Elena tried her best to make things better for them. I'm sorry about everything, boys." He rose, brushing off his pants, and patted each of our sweating heads before going inside.

Max and I looked at each other, baffled and amazed. Ivan said softly, "So did I do it?"

Max cried, "You didn't! You heard him, Ivan! That's *great*!"

"She's still dead, Max."

Realizing his insensitivity, Max apologized. "I'm an idiot."

"But, Ivan, you don't have to feel guilty anymore! You should feel better about *that*," I said.

"I guess," he said dully. "But what about the spider toxins?"

"He said *everybody* had them!" I practically shouted. "Forget about it, Ivan!"

Brickie's remark regarding Gellert's family struck me as summing everything up: *Elena tried her best to make things better.* Weird for this to be coming from Brickie, who had had reservations about Elena all along, but then I remembered them happily dancing together at the Fiesta. Elena had certainly made things better for Ivan and me. I grieved for myself, but how Ivan was going to get along without her in the world I could not imagine.

15

But get along we had to. In the weeks following Elena's death, we'd returned to school and resumed those rituals: trudging back and forth to Rosemary, learning long division and practicing multiplication tables and cursive writing in our despised Palmer Method handbooks, eating the thirty-five-cent lunches served up in our smelly cafeteria, playing kickball at recess (and losing without Gellert), doing or pretending to do our homework, and hanging out together before bedtime, which, with fall, had become a very short respite. Ivan was not the same—woebegone and more quiet even than he'd been before.

I received a letter from my mother, condolences about Elena for me, Max, and Ivan but also with the wonderful news that she'd be coming home "for good" very soon. She and my dad seemed to have settled their legal issue, and Dad took me and the boys to a movie. Max and I wanted to see *Plan 9 from Outer Space,* but Dad thought we should see something funny, so we saw *The Shaggy Dog.* It was okay—a kid turns into a dog. Ivan said he wished it were him. Liz came home from Holton-Arms one weekend and helped us paint Elena's swing a shiny, vibrant red, a shade approximating Sports Car. Beatriz painted an angel on the back. We didn't ask Josef for permission; we just did it.

The Fabulous Family Fiesta had been a success, insofar as Kees and Piet did invite us—Max included—to swim in their pool. We enjoyed a few weeks of fun until it got too cold, and they drained it for the winter. Then Mr. Chappaqua took us, packed like sardines, for a spin in the Messerschmitt. We didn't give a damn about being traitors. Josephine hired us to rake the leaves in the Pond Lady's yard, but our enthusiasm for the pond and spiders had cooled, to say the least. Miss Braddock died, and we thought about breaking in to see the dollhouse while it was still there, but our enthusiasm for breaking in had cooled as well.

The world continued being the weirdest place on earth, and the Cold War kept getting hotter. We learned in our *Weekly Reader*s that Khrushchev was visiting the United States and had gotten mad because he wasn't allowed to go to Disneyland. Brickie told us that Khrushchev said that the mayor of Los Angeles had "tried to let out a little fart, and instead he shit his pants," which naturally amused us. Eisenhower was going to try to smooth things over by entertaining Khrushchev at Camp David, out in the Catoctin hills, not too far from us.

On an Indian summer afternoon, Ivan and I were riding with Dimma in her Cadillac to the Mann Farm for the annual Democratic picnic. Dimma was going to support John F. Kennedy for president in the upcoming election, because he "has class, and is smart, and he's wealthy, so he won't be using the presidency to make money," but I thought that she really liked him because he was young and handsome and had a glamorous wife who wore French clothes. I didn't blame her.

As we were traveling out Wisconsin Avenue, suddenly cars were pulling over and people were spilling onto the median. Dimma said excitedly, "Boys! It must be Eisenhower coming back from Camp David!" She pulled over and we joined everyone. Rolling very slowly toward us was a convertible limousine. In the backseat sat two old guys with bald heads: Ike *and* Nikita.

People were shouting and waving, and then there they were, next to us. We were so close to Khrushchev we could see the warts on his face. Ivan shouted, *"Dasvidaniya!"* The potato face turned, and he smiled and waved to Ivan.

I yelled, "*Khrushchev* waved at you!" Ivan beamed, the first happy smile I'd seen from him in forever.

We were so excited and so was Dimma, but I couldn't understand exactly why—wasn't this America's greatest enemy? Returning to the Caddy, Dimma said, "Well, wasn't *that* something! I'm so glad you boys got to see them!"

I had a chance to quiz Brickie about the event that evening when we were in the kitchen having an early Bachelor Night. He hated Khrushchev, but admitted that seeing an important figure like that—*two* important figures—didn't happen every day. "Whatever he is now, he was an ally and a war hero," Brickie said, flipping our sizzling burgers. "One day you'll be telling your grandchildren about it. *If* he hasn't blown us up by then."

"Well, I won't have children *or* grandchildren, because I'm not getting married."

"Oh, I suspect you'll change your mind about that."

"I might have married Elena." I think that was the first time I'd said her name since she'd died, and it gave me a pang. "But she's the only one."

"I can understand your feeling that way. Elena was a lovely woman." Brickie was quiet for a minute. "She was . . . a complex person, John."

"What do you mean?"

"That man who picked her up from your Fiesta? That was Camilo Cienfuegos, a dangerous Cuban revolutionary."

"So?" Then Elena's words popped out of my mouth: "Not everyone in Cuba is bad. They're trying to help poor people there."

"They're *Communists,* John. And Elena helped them. She wasn't just aiding refugees."

This stunned me, as if he'd told me that Elena was an alien from Mars. "You mean . . . she was a *spy*?"

"Not exactly. She was . . . *an agent of influence,* entertaining foreign men who could give significant money to the revolutionary cause. She also entertained American officials who might tell her things—secrets—about our government, which she may then have passed on to people like Camilo Cienfuegos. She was probably going to be arrested before long. But this is America, not Russia, and you can't just arrest people without probable cause."

I said, "What do you mean—*entertaining*? Like at parties?"

"You'll understand when you're older." That again. "And I want you to promise not to tell Ivan any of this. He doesn't need to know. Or he may know already, poor boy. *You* need to know because I think you're old enough to understand that people are not always what they seem. You musn't be too trusting on the face of things."

"That's exactly what *Elena* told us." I hated hearing all this, but couldn't help asking, "What happened to the guy on the motorcycle?"

"He got back to Cuba, we assume. And Elena had intended to go with him. The police stopped them for speeding, and that's why Elena came home that night. But they didn't realize who Camilo was, and later let him go. But it wouldn't surprise me if Camilo . . . disappears before long. Damn—I forgot about our hash browns."

I was confused and angry and sick of hearing bad things about Elena, which I wasn't sure I believed anyway. I ate my burger in silence.

Brickie sat down with his plate and a Scotch. "And not a word of this to Ivan, or anybody else. Understand?" I didn't answer and decided that I wasn't going to speak to Brickie anymore. Or at least not until tomorrow.

After eating, I went over to Ivan's backyard. The day had been so sunny and beautiful, but the sky had suddenly turned leaden, and a fierce, cold wind had blown in, heaving the huge oak branches up and down in slow motion, while their leaves waved furiously like little hands until they fell with the gusts, brilliant scraps of color against the gray sky.

We became excited, the brisk air telling us that it would soon be Halloween. "Let's be Eisenhower and Khrushchev for Trick or Treat!" Ivan said. To please him, I offered to be Khrushchev. Ivan said, "We'll put a stocking on your head to make you bald, and make Play-Doh warts for your face! You can carry a shoe and bang it and say, 'We will bury you!' at every house!" It was great to see Ivan happy.

We whirled around in the wind and leaves till dark, then Brickie called me in. Ivan became serious again. "This cold and wind will definitely kill all the spiders now, if there are any still around."

"I thought we were through with spiders," I said.

"We are. I'm just sad about them dying."

"There's always next summer," I said.

"Yeah, there's always next summer."

But by New Year's, some of our neighbors—the Shreves and the De Haans—had moved away from Connors Lane. And not long after that, Josef was posted to the Philippines, taking Ivan with him, and this smashed my broken heart all over again.

Max had begun to draw away, spending more time with friends from Hebrew school and getting serious about playing basketball. We were still close friends, but I was aware of the age gap between us getting wider. Beatriz and I stayed good friends, too, but she was sucked further into the world of girls and had even less time to spend hanging around, although she and Max, of all people, did start walking together to Doc's and talking on the phone. I felt jealous and betrayed and started calling them Popeye and Olive Oyl, which didn't sit well with them, so I gave that up.

My mother did come back from St. Elizabeths, and I was very happy about that, at least until she started dating. Brickie and Dimma stayed on with us, maybe to keep an eye on things. My father married Carline and got a steady job managing a restaurant. Slutcheon got sent off to Charlotte Hall, after all—no more looking over our shoulders. And, as Brickie predicted, just before Halloween, Camilo Cienfuegos did probably disappear over the Straits of Florida.

Of course, nothing was the same without Ivan and Elena. Ivan and I wrote to each other a few times, and I learned he was sent to a boarding school in London, and I was glad about that. I didn't tell him about Max and Beatriz ditching me, which would only have made him worry. The last time he'd written, he sent a little purple drawing of a pirate vinegaroon, and all the note said was "Your blood brother, Ivan." I never saw or heard from him again.

Life went on, as it will. That summer stayed with me, surreal footage that seemed more and more like a movie with every passing day. We kids were merely flotsam and jetsam on the crazy river that life is, and even though we'd hit the whitewater of the adult world, we'd come up, bobbing along, but never again quite so buoyant. I can see that much of the drama was just Washington, where things can change fast, weirdness and treachery can prevail, people and things are neither what they seem nor what they are said to be, and the world's issues and events are played out in neighborhoods like Connors Lane. And everybody is forever moving on. Eventually, I would, too, although wherever I happened to be, if I heard "The Twelfth of Never" or glimpsed a beautiful spiderweb, my heart bumped up hard against the indelible memories of our darling Elena and my dearest friend, Ivan.

Author's Note

Although most of the characters in this book are fictional, I want to mention a few who are not. I took some small liberties imagining these characters' parts in this novel.

James Hampton is one of the great American artists of the twentieth century. He was born in Elloree, South Carolina, in 1909, the son of a gospel singer, and went to Washington in 1928, later serving in the Army Air Forces in the 385th Aviation Squadron in Saipan and Guam, receiving a Bronze Star. He returned to Washington after the war and worked as a janitor for the General Services Administration until his death in 1964. During that time, in a garage on Seventh Street NW, he secretly created the masterpiece *The Throne of the Third Heaven of the Nations' Millennium General Assembly,* a spectacular assemblage based on biblical prophesy and visions, with elements of African spiritualism. I remember well when, after his death, *The Washington Post* reported on the astounding discovery of *The Throne,* which is now at the Smithsonian American Art Museum.

Ezra Pound (1885–1972) was an expat American and major figure in modernist poetry. While living in Italy, he became controversial, embracing Fascism and supporting Mussolini and Hitler, which eventually led to his arrest and incarceration by American forces for treason. For a few weeks, he lived in a steel cage, causing his mental breakdown, after which he resided at St. Elizabeths in Washington for twelve years and was released in 1958. Ironically, during his incarceration, he was awarded the first Bollingen Prize by the Library of Congress for his *Pisan Cantos*. It is said in my family that my paternal grandmother and maternal great-grandmother, both Italian immigrants, spent time in St. Elizabeths in the 1940s or 1950s, and I've often fantasized about their paths having crossed Pound's there.

Lieutenant Jacob Beser (1921–1992) was from Baltimore. His family was Jewish, and he was especially committed to defeating Hitler. He worked in Los Alamos on the Manhattan Project and was a radar specialist aboard the *Enola Gay* and the *Bockscar*—the only person to have served on both 1945 atomic missions to Japan. He has said that he felt no remorse over his part in those missions: "One must consider the context of the times." Beser was awarded the Silver Star and other medals for his service.

Camilo Cienfuegos, born in 1932 in Havana, was close to Castro and Che Guevara and, like Che, a charismatic Cuban revolutionary who was one of the top guerrilla commanders in the struggle against dictator Fulgencio Batista. He also had studied art, played on Castro's baseball team, Barbudos, and visited the United States twice, working in New York, San Francisco, Chicago, and Miami. After Castro's victory in 1959, Camilo headed Cuba's armed forces until his mysterious disappearance over the Straits of Florida. His plane was never recovered. Camilo remains popular and is memorialized all over Cuba.

I would also like to acknowledge a few books I consulted while writing this novel: *Field Guide to North American Insects and Spiders,* The National Audubon Society, Alfred A. Knopf, 1980; *Naturalist,* Edward O. Wilson, Island Press, 1994; *Camilo: eternamente presente,* Edimirta Ortega Guzman, compiler, Oficina de Publicaciones del Consejo de Estado, 2014; and *The Bughouse: The Poetry, Politics, and Madness of Ezra Pound,* Daniel Swift, Farrar, Straus & Giroux, 2017.

Acknowledgments

Thanks to so many for help and reading: Claiborne, Marian, and Norma Barksdale, Beckett Howorth IV, Sam Johnston, Po Hannah, Katie Blount, Amanda Hewitt, Darrell Crawford and David McConnell, Debra Winger, Babe Howard, Anne Rapp, Kathryn Wood, Jennifer Ackerman, Bill Cusumano, B. A. Fennelly, Curtis Wilkie, Jack Pendarvis, Gary Fisketjon, Joey Lauren Adams, Lee Durkee, Elizabeth Dollarhide, Jeff Dennis, Tom Verich, Bernard Kuria, Kyle McGrevey, Kathy and Dan Woodliff, Homer Best, David Howorth, Biff Grimes, Patty Orama, and Tim Kosel at easysonglicensing.com. Thanks to my homey, Frank Rich, for a copy of the flabbergasting book *Washington Confidential,* and to my mom, Claire Johnston; dad, George Neumann; and brother, Rick Neumann, for childhood inspiration. Thanks to Chris Wait and Barbara Epler at New Directions; my friends Phin and Liam Percy, who provided their artistic talents; and to the P.P.P. at the Pig, and the B.D.S. at the Grocery, for keeping me laffing. As always, thanks to my husband, Richard, for advice and *putting up.* And tons of gratitude is due to my crafty agent, Lisa Bankoff, who gets things off the ground; to my incredibly hardworking, smart editor, Lee Boudreaux; and to everybody at Doubleday, especially the eagle-eyed Cara Reilly, copy editor Amy Edelman, designer Michael Collica, production editor Victoria Pearson, publicist Todd Doughty, and sales reps Julie Kurland and Jess Pearson.

ABOUT THE AUTHOR

Lisa Howorth was born in Washington, DC, where her family has lived for four generations. She is a former librarian and the author of the novel *Flying Shoes.* She has written on art, travel, dogs, and music for the *Oxford American* and *Garden & Gun,* among other publications. Howorth lives in Oxford, Mississippi, where she and her husband, Richard, cofounded Square Books in 1979.